THE BRAMPTON MUSKETEERS

Robina Brooks

Copyright Written Work: © Robina Brooks 2022
Copyright Images: © Pen & Ink Designs 2022

Publisher: Pen & Ink Designs 2022

ISBN: 978-1-915086-06-8

DEDICATION

I dedicate this book to women everywhere but especially to those ladies who were part of my early life. Your experiences gave me the ideas upon which to base the stories contained within this book.

You were all strong, unique young girls in your own right and I believe and hope that you will all have grown into even stronger mature women.

All though we have lost touch over the years I have never forgotten any one of you or the lasting impression you left on me.

Robina Brooks

MESSAGE FROM THE AUTHOR

Dear Reader,

Robina Brooks is a pseudonym.

Having wanted to experiment with a new style of writing, the content within this book is a contrast to the other works I have created and as such, I didn't want to muddy the waters.

Whilst the stories contained within the book are a figment of my imagination they are based on some factual events that occurred to people I knew in my early years. The names of course are fictitious. The question though, is whether you can determine fact from fiction as the events are in the main true to real life.

I do hope you will enjoy reading about the Brampton Musketeers' journey as they travel through those times in their lives that this book portrays.

However, if you have been affected in any way because of these stories please remember that you can overcome. There is always hope for achieving your life's dreams if you only have faith in yourself.

Good luck and All the Best.

Robina Brooks

CONTENTS

FOREWORD

As Susie looked at the pile of blue envelopes she wondered once again what had she been thinking in wanting to organise such an event as a school reunion. Her birthday had passed recently and for the first time in her eighteen years of marriage, Ted had forgotten it. He had looked slightly sheepish when Debbie, their daughter, had made a big fuss of Susie, bringing her flowers, a big card, and a box of chocolates. Ted's excuse had been that he had been too busy due to the pressure of work. Susie felt different.

Returning home that evening, after the three of them had been out for a meal at a local restaurant, Susie had gone to bed alone. The meal had been Ted's way of trying to make amends for no gift or card. Susie had pretended it didn't matter, but his forgetfulness had hurt her this time. They hadn't spoken for three days. Well, they hadn't spoken because Ted had disappeared the next morning and not returned for three days. 'That had been him pouring salt on the wounds,' she thought.

Looking at the envelopes again, Susie thought about School – 'Those halcyon days when we tended to say we were bored or fed-up? Or were we?' She supposed that as people got older we would all have looked back at those days; from the nursery school stage to the primary years, onto and through those heady senior years. Even perhaps, beyond school to college or university. In reality, most of those years were probably happy, yet some were the opposite. As such, there will be many who may say 'that school wasn't for me' – 'that they didn't enjoy their time there.'

And yet, strangely enough, many of our long-time friends, "not to mention future spouses," she said out loud, were sometimes met and made whilst at school. Friends whom we spent many hours with. Who we would often find ourselves laughing, crying, or just chatting with. They were the friends we promised to always stay in touch with. And yet, whilst some of those friendships continued into our grown-up years, many others soon disappeared, much to our regret.

Sighing, Susie, picked the pile of envelopes up, then grabbing her handbag she went out the door and headed down the street towards the local post office. Once the invitations were posted the deed was done. The reunion was now a foregone conclusion – 'Well, that is if people agree to come to the event,' thought Susie.

THE PAST

'The past is the set of all events that occurred before a given point in time.' Wikipedia

In our past life, we will all have had something happen that will have affected us. Most times we will have enjoyed the experiences. Remembering the happy times, although there are probably lots of incidents which we will choose to forget. No one ever told us that our lives would be easy, nor should they be. However, as far as we know, the life we lead is the only one we have, so we should make the most of it. Enjoying the ups, while doing our level best to cope, and come to terms with, the downs.

Part of living our life includes meeting new people and creating friendships. Sometimes these friendships last a lifetime, whilst others just disappear into the ether – here today, gone tomorrow. But that's the way life is. All that you do, all those you meet and all the places you visit are just part of life's rich and varied tapestry. Your life's tapestry.

Most people will have happy memories of their developing years. And whilst they may have argued with their siblings, if they had them, where those siblings are no longer present then that interaction will be missed. The same can be said of our friends.

But what happens when those friends or siblings let you down? When they force you to look at their motives, at your way of life, even to leave home, and all because of their words, their feelings, or actions. All this will affect you the person. What happens within your life becomes a part of your make-up. Helping you as it shows you how to develop into a functioning human being. The question is what type of person will you be.

Let's start with Melinda and the event that led her to decide which path to choose, to follow, and the life it led her to…

MELINDA

Trust deceived…

"Come on, Melinda, you'll be late for school."

"I'm coming, Mum," yelled Melinda as she grabbed her school bag, before racing down the stairs of the small terraced house where she lived with her brother, mom, and dad.

"Ready, Mum," she said. Then picking up her lunch pack she called out 'see ya' and was out the door as quickly as possible, last being seen racing away.

Her mother stood watching her daughter running down the street. Melinda had blonde hair and was thin but she also had long legs for a fifteen-year-old. A bright kid, her mother hoped she would get a better chance at life than she had ever had. Sighing, she turned back into the house. As she did a piercing pain shot through her lower chest. 'Damned indigestion,' she thought.

As Melinda ran along she was glad to be out of the house. She had always enjoyed going to school, especially as it gave her the chance to play her favourite sport – netball. Being taller than any of the other girls gave her an advantage. Also, the fact she could run, having a long stride because of her long legs meant she had soon become a much-needed part of the team. Yes, Melinda loved going to school but, apart from being with her mum, she hated being at home.

Her brother was a selfish kid. He was four years older than her and took every opportunity to annoy, tease and abuse her. She had never told her mum that he had started coming into her room when she was about eleven. She had started to grow small breasts back then so he had decided he wanted to look at and touch them. When she complained, he told her she would do as she was told or he would get her into trouble. Even when she threatened to tell their mum what he was doing, he said she wouldn't believe her, besides their dad would only hit her for lying. Despite her not wanting him to come near her Melinda found herself letting him touch her. The touching of her breasts had gone on for a few weeks. Then he had stopped, just as suddenly as he had started. Melinda was relieved. However, there was worse yet to come.

About two months after her thirteenth birthday, her parents decided to go visit some relatives. They wouldn't be back until the following day. They were going out for the night and as her brother was seventeen and she was now thirteen they felt they were old enough to be left on their own. Melinda didn't think anything about it, expecting her brother to watch

TV while she would stay in her room. Her brother had asked if his friend could stay for a while and their dad had said yes, probably thinking the more the merrier when it came to looking after Melinda.

It was about ten o'clock when Melinda realised something was wrong. The door to her bedroom had been opened. Although quietly, it was the sound of giggling which had alerted her that someone was in her room. As she started to sit up, her brother and his friend pounced. Melinda being half asleep yelled, "You get out now or I'm going to tell mum and dad about you."

The two boys laughed, as they bounced on the bed, landing on top of her.

"So, Tom, do you want to look?" her brother asked.

Tom just smiled and nodded his head.

His response caused her brother to start pulling at the bedding, saying, "Come on, Mel, Tom wants to look at your titties. Show him, or else."

Melinda was horrified and started fighting. This was her brother. How could he do this to her?

"Bitch," snarled her brother, and he hit her across the face. "Come on, Tom, help me get her undressed."

Despite her putting up a struggle, Melinda, was too weak, being quickly overpowered by the two boys.

Tears streamed down Melinda's face, but struggling as hard as she did, she still couldn't stop him from doing what he wanted with her.

"Come and have a feel," Tom told her brother.

"Naw, you have a go first. I'll get her later. I'm going to go watch TV and have another drink. I'll leave you two love birds to have some fun. Enjoy yourself, Tom," and moving away from the bed he was ready to leave the room.

Stopping in the doorway, he said, "No penetration. That's for me to do first," and he laughed as he went down the stairs.

Melinda started struggling again, pleading with Tom with her eyes not to do this, but to let her go. He, however, was too busy enjoying himself. He had always wanted to touch a girl on her private bits and now he had his chance.

Time seemed to stand still for Melinda. Tom was certainly getting his plate full, touching her as much as he wanted. Suddenly he stopped. Going towards the bedroom door, he listened. It seemed her brother was enthralled in watching a dirty movie. Closing the door he lodged a chair under the door handle. Then he started stripping off. All the playing with Melinda had given him a hard-on and he needed to release the pressure. To hell with what his mate said. She was ripe and he was ready.

Slowly he climbed onto the bed, grinning all the time. Because Melinda had long legs it was easy to pull her down towards the bottom of the bed and slide himself between her legs. Laying on top of her, he said, "Now, why should your brother have all the fun, when I've got a nice present for you. Mel, you're gonna like this," and without waiting any longer he began pushing himself into her.

Melinda couldn't scream out loud as the gag in her mouth stopped her. The pain didn't seem to be stopping as Tom pushed in and out of her with such a force. "Wow, you feel good. All nice and tight." In and out, on and on he went until a banging came at the door.

"Tom, you bastard. Open this bloody door? You'd better not be doing her. She's mine to do, not yours. Open this door, you wanker."

It was on that note, that Tom reached his orgasm.

Climbing off the bed, he was panting. Slipping on his pants he opened the bedroom door.

Her brother was angry. "You bastard," he yelled. "Get the hell out of here."

Tom grinned, picking up his clothes. As he left, he said, "Same time next week? We could share her; you know she's a nice tight fuck."

After Tom had left, her brother returned to Melinda's room. He looked at his sister laid spreadeagled on the bed. Tears were streaming down her face. Grinning at her he turned the light out and left her as she was.

Melinda sighed with relief that the ordeal was over, but she was still tied to the bed. Surely he would come back and untie her soon? Being exhausted she unwillingly closed her eyes and fell asleep.

* * * * *

The movement of the bed and her brother's hard cock pushing in and out of her slowly brought Melinda back to the surface. How long he had been riding her she didn't know but it seemed as if he was in her for the long haul. Melinda lay like a dead woman. Her mind and body having separated from each other.

After some time, her brother finally came inside her and being satiated he climbed off her. Looking at her, he sighed, then undid the ties around her hands.

Pulling the gag from her mouth she cried, "You evil bastard. You let that dirtbag molest and rape me, and then you did the same. I'm going to tell dad what an evil bastard you are," and she burst into tears. "I hope you've made me pregnant then I can get you both into trouble with the police."

Grabbing her hair, her brother looked into her eyes, whispering harshly, "You open your mouth about this and so help me I'll give you to every lad I know. They'll love fucking the hell out of you. No, Mel, you'll keep your big mouth shut or else. From now on, you keep your door unlocked. So if I want to touch or fuck you, then you will let me, or else."

"Oh, no, I won't. You ever come near me again, I'll kill you. You bastard. Now, get out of my room or so help me I will tell mum and dad, and… grannie, and… the… the police about what happened here tonight. And, you can tell Tom, if I ever see his face in this house again, I'm going do the same to him as well. I'm sure his parents will love to know what their darling boy gets up to on a night out. Raping young underage girls. Now get out of my room."

After her brother had left her room, Melinda unfastened her feet then went into the bathroom to clean herself up. She was pretty sore down below and there was blood mixed with the semen spread over the top of her legs. She would set her alarm and get up early to take a bath before their parents came home.

She knew she should go to the doctor but he would ask questions. Maybe one of her school friends, one of the Brampton Musketeers, could help her. They might know what she could do to ensure she was okay. The question was, who could she trust?

The following day it took Melinda sometime before she plucked up the courage to tell someone what had happened to her. Strangely the one person she chose was the most unexpected. It was Coleen. She was Irish and Catholic, so shouldn't have known about the stuff that had happened to Melinda.

However, as it turned out, Coleen, who was over from Ireland and staying with her aunt, knew just who to ask for help - her aunt. It seemed that lady worked for a local young mother's organisation so Coleen asked her what Melinda should do.

Thanks to Coleen's aunty, Melinda was seen privately by a specialist nurse from the organisation. She gave Melinda the 'morning after pill' just to make sure she wasn't pregnant. They also tested her for any sexual diseases - again, luckily, she got the all-clear.

Apart from the horrific experience, Melinda was thankful that she had gotten off so lightly. Physically that was. However, the mental effects would take a long time to disappear and they would affect her for the rest of her life.

In the meantime, she watched her brother like a hawk. Locking her bedroom door at night. She had even started carrying a pen knife on her person. Although she wasn't sure what use it would be, or whether or not she could use it, she thought that still, it might help. As regards her brother, when no one was watching she would take the knife out and threaten to cut his throat with it. Eventually, he got the message, staying away from her thereafter.

After what had happened Melinda couldn't wait to leave school and get away from the area. She was determined to leave the district, wanting to find somewhere new to live where no one knew her.

MELINDA

Leaving home…

Stepping down from the train, Melinda breathed a sigh of relief. She knew she was stepping into the unknown. She was seventeen years old, having celebrated her birthday four months before leaving school.

During the last few weeks of school, Melinda had sent some photos off to a few London modelling agencies. She had managed to save some money from the odd jobs she'd done during the summer school breaks, and she still had the bank account with the inheritance money in from her Grandfather who had passed away a few years ago. It wasn't a lot, but enough to last for a few weeks. If she didn't get a modelling job then she would have to find something else until she did.

Luckily, her aunt on her mother's side lived on the outskirts of London so she had somewhere to stay. Arriving at the house, Melinda was amazed at the size of the place. To her, it looked like a palace, especially when compared to their home. Her Aunt had agreed to take her in because Melinda had told her she had had a big argument with her dad.

Later, she would tell her what had happened. Her

aunt was horrified, saying she should have told her mother, but Melinda told her, "Mum's not well, and I didn't want to worry her. I got checked over by a special nurse but, once school was done, I couldn't stay in the house any longer." Understanding this, her aunt had agreed Melinda could stay as long as she wanted. Besides, she had never gotten on that well with her sister and she hated her brother-in-law so was happy to help.

* * * * *

Unfortunately for Melinda, the modelling jobs had never really materialised. However, over time Melinda had learnt that her Aunt was in fact a high-end call girl - well, a madame really. Her home had been bought with the money she'd made running a very posh brothel for the last twenty years. But her standard of living was down to her being kept by a titled gentleman for many years.

Little did Melinda realise that this too would also become her future.

* * * * *

Over the next couple of years, Melinda began to learn the brothel trade. Not that her aunt had had any intention of allowing her niece to ever become a prostitute or a call-girl like she had been. Especially after what had happened with her brother and his friend. In the end, the pair agreed that Melinda would become a hostess in the brothel bar. This would entail her looking after the more upmarket clientele until their room, and their special lady was ready to service them. In some respects, Melinda was happy with this role as the memories of her rape were still quite raw and she didn't think she could have handled a man, any man, touching her so intimately.

However, over time Melinda began developing a new life for herself. Her reputation as a hostess began to grow, and soon her role changed to that of becoming an escort; someone who accompanied a gentleman to special or important events. Such was her reputation that she became one of the most sort after escort ladies to be seen out and about with. Even though she didn't sleep with any of the men she 'dated' she was still in high demand. This meant she lived in style and wore expensive clothes. She was also fortunate enough to be able to be selective in the type of men she spent her time with. And as her rates were high, you had to be pretty rich to spend time in her company.

MELINDA

A new life…

Melinda had been in London some ten years or so when her dear aunt passed away. It proved to be one of the best-attended funerals of the year, if not the decade. Anyone who was someone of standing was there. Including the hoity-toity of society, titled gentlemen, and even members of the Police Constabulary, not to mention more ladies of the night than had ever gathered in one place at any one time. All it had needed was Dolly Parton singing that song 'The Chicken Ranch' to complete the scene. Still, Melinda was pleased that they had given her aunt the best send-off to brothel heaven they could. The follow-up party or wake lasted three days and nights. In celebration of her aunt's long-standing in the community, all the girls were free for the whole of the party. It might have cost Melinda a small fortune but it sealed her position as her aunt's replacement and earned the girls some extra pocket money.

A few weeks after the funeral, Melinda gathered the workers and other staff together.

"I've decided that as much as my aunt had taste, this place needs bringing up to date. I have therefore decided that we are going to refurbish the house and as such we are closing the doors Sunday night."

"What, you got to be kidding. What are we supposed to do?" asked Clarissa, one of the longest-standing regulars. "Hell, Melinda, I'm too old to go on the streets."

Holding her hand up, Melinda called for them to be quiet. Once silence reigned, she said, "I have bought the two small houses next door. The renovations have been ongoing for weeks now and come Sunday they should be finished. We will be moving into there for a few weeks while the builders start refurbishing this place. You will all take three weeks paid leave, at my expense, and... when you return, this place will have doubled and will have been renamed. I am going to open a nightclub. I have been promised all the necessary licences, etc. So, ladies what do you say?"

Of course, all the girls were delighted with the news, especially as they were getting a paid holiday.

* * * * *

Four weeks later, The Pentagon Club opened its doors for the first time. Sat in the corner of the bar was Lady Melinda, owner, and madame, who watched closely all those who entered through the doors. Not red ones like most brothel doors might be painted, but more of a selective purple with other décor to complement the colour. It looked more upmarket than it originally had, and with the extension into the two houses next door, The Pentagon Club was to become the best and most famous 'house of ill-repute' London would ever see.

As the months passed, Melinda would meet many people and over time she would become the toast of the London brothel/club scene. Would she bury the memories of her teenage years or meet the man of her dreams only time would tell…

PHILLIPA

Unrest at home…

Phillipa or Pip as she was called had always felt she lived a normal life. Well, as normal as she knew or thought was possible for her family. Even if it wasn't. Her family consisted of herself (Pip), her sister, brother, and her mother and father. Oh, and her grandmother (Dad's mum) as well. Grannie had come to live with the family not long after Phillipa had been born. Being the youngest, hers had apparently been the hardest birth for her mother, with the whole experience having left her mother determined to never have any more children. Sticking to her guns on that one, she had quickly declared herself a poorly woman whenever it came to her husband's marital rights.

At first, Phillipa's father had been understanding, after all the baby had been a breach birth and his wife had been in labour for at least fifteen hours. However, over time he had started to become frustrated. The children and Grannie would often hear the arguments coming from their parents' bedroom as her father demanded his wife 'service' him. She, however, had always fought back, categorically refusing him. Finally, he had stood enough and started having an affair. In the beginning, it had been purely sex. He was a man after all and, as he plainly put it, a man has needs and desires. As far as he was concerned, if his wife wouldn't see to him, then he would find it elsewhere. And he did.

By the time Pip was aged about five, her father had had a regular string of lady friends. It seemed her mother didn't mind. Or at least she appeared not to. She would spend her days cooking, cleaning, and caring for the children. To Pip, this seemed normal. Her father was happy. Her grannie was happy because her son was happy. Her sibling appeared happy. Even her mother seemed happy.

And yet, she wasn't. If Phillipa had been older she may have questioned why her mother wasn't happy. Had she done so, maybe she would have realised that her mother had gone from being a wife, who was loved and cared for, to being just a housekeeper.

But hadn't she got what she wanted? No more sex with her husband. Whilst he was being serviced elsewhere, he was leaving her alone. The problem was, with her husband being treated special elsewhere, it meant that her mother now missed out on her husband's loving and caring nature. He was giving all that to another woman. Oh yes, he was happy, and always smiling, while Phillipa's mother was sad and extremely unhappy.

This state of affairs would continue right up until after Phillipa left school.

PHILLIPA

Time for a reckoning...

It was at her eighteenth birthday party that her mother had finally sprung her big surprise. That evening, she had walked into the hall where the party was being held, dressed up to the nines and looking like a model. Not only that, she was accompanied by a tall younger-looking man. Her father had looked at her in both amazement and shock.

Finally finding his tongue, he had gone over to his wife, and asked, "What the hell are you doing? And who the hell is this?"

His wife, smiling, had turned to face him. Then in a low voice, she had said, "It's called tit for tat, dear. Did you really think it would be alright for you to go out and fuck whoever you wanted without ever considering that I might actually be suffering? No, you didn't, did you? No. All you ever thought about was you, your dick, and where you could put it. Well, my dear, I don't need your dick anymore, because I've found a nice big, hard one that satisfies me a lot better than yours ever did, so why don't you run along and go play with all your little floosies. Go on, go and enjoy yourself," and she turned away.

Phillipa, who had caught the end of the conversation, was shocked. This was her mother talking dirty to her father. But, what was worse, was how he just stood there saying nothing; although he did look about ready to explode.

Seeing her, Pip's mother said, "Pip, sweetheart, I'm so glad to see you. Now my darling, I just wanted to wish you a Happy Birthday before I leave. You have a lovely life and please, my sweetie, don't make the same stupid mistakes I have. Get out into the big world and see what it has to offer you. Chow, my darling," and on that note, she turned to leave.

As she turned away, Phillipa said, "Leave! Mother, what do you mean, leave? It's my birthday party. Where are you going?"

"Darling, I'm leaving home. I've had enough of being a bloody slave to you, your brother, your sister, your cheating father, and especially your bloody lazy grannie. Enough is enough. Listen my darling, you go find yourself a nice young man. Travel the world and fuck him senseless, just don't get pregnant. Kids will be the bane of your life. Happy birthday, darling," and kissing a shocked Phillipa her mother turned and left the room. The young man she had with her following behind, grinning from ear to ear.

PHILLIPA

Romance in the air...

About two years later, Phillipa changed jobs, going from working in an office to that of a travel company. It was while working there that she met Roland Fitzpatrick. He was a regular client who travelled a great deal so he used their company to arrange all his travel arrangements. Roland was smooth and slick. Smooth in his dress and ways, and slick in his talk. The moment he spotted Phillipa he had decided he wanted her. After all, she was thin, quite pretty, and sexy-looking.

Roland soon turned the charm on, asking her out on a date during his second visit to the store. They hit it off straight away. He asked her if she liked to travel. She said she had never gone anywhere. Asking her, why not, she explained she was completing a secretarial course, but maybe one day she would like to visit somewhere foreign. He had just booked a trip to South America, saying he would see her when he returned.

* * * * *

About two months later, as Phillipa exited the building of the secretarial course for the last time she was surprised to find Roland waiting for her. Unexpectedly, he took her in his arms and kissed her quite soundly, telling her how much he had missed her. That was the start of their relationship.

Over the next few weeks, Roland turned the charm button too high and within a short period of time, he had Phillipa in his bed, being delighted when he discovered she was a virgin and he was her first. The sex for both of them was good. But Phillipa hadn't forgotten what her mother had told her. Don't get pregnant. So even though she was enjoying the sex, she made sure she was well protected.

About six months later, Roland suggested they tour the world. The idea being that they travel to as many countries as they could. They would have some money to take with them, placing a small fund in a bank for emergencies. And to support themselves they would find work wherever they landed. He would do manual labour, whilst Phillipa could use her secretarial skills. Although the idea frighted Phillipa, it also excited her. Why shouldn't she go? After all, she would be with Roland. She would be safe because he would protect her. He had told her so. And so, with the decision made they set off for India.

PHILLIPA

All roads lead home...

Travelling across Europe, Phillipa and Roland found their way easy. Deciding to take their time they worked odd jobs where they could to keep their funds topped up, as well as sleeping in youth hostels or cheap hotels. Being together is probably what protected Phillipa more than she realised.

After about six months they managed to get a boat ride from Malta to Cyprus where they spent a good couple of months enjoying the island. Once they were refreshed they became crew members on a boat that took them down towards the Suez Canal. Being so close to Israel the pair chose to live in a Kibbutz for some time where they worked hard, being part of the community for close to eighteen months. Eventually, Roland found the constrictive nature of the complex too much, so decided they would move on to somewhere new.

Eventually, they arrived in the Philippines, having crossed India, Cambodia, and Vietnam before boarding another boat across the South China Seas. They were like hippies. Living and working alongside the locals. At first, Phillipa had found it strenuous but over time she had managed to adapt and soon began to love their nomadic lifestyle. She felt free. Each day they worked, cooked some food, washed in a local stream or river, and finally slept together in a hut. And each night Roland made mad passionate love to her, telling her how beautiful and sexy she was, and how much he loved her.

Their next stops included Indonesia and Papua New Guinea before the pair finally decided to head for Australia. To Phillipa, it was like returning to some form of normality. For a start they spoke a language she understood but still, they retained their independent freedom. Unfortunately, it wasn't to last.

* * * * *

About five months into their touring of Australia, Roland received a communiqué from England. His father had suffered a mental breakdown and Roland was urgently needed back home to run the family business. His mother was stressing out big time. They were left with little option but to answer her distress call and return to the UK.

Phillipa had been very tempted to tell Roland to go home alone. That she would stay and wait for him in Australia, but she somehow knew that he wouldn't return. Perhaps he sensed her reluctance to leave as he did the one thing Phillipa least expected. He asked her to marry him. With his declaration of love and passion,

Phillipa felt left with little option but to accept his proposal and return to England with him.

It was going to be a decision she would always regret.

COLEEN

Meeting one's maker...

"Hurray up, there, Shauna," called Sinead to her sister. "You'll miss the bus, girl."

"Aye, now don't ye be worrying about me, Sinead. You be thinking o'your-sen," said Shauna as she pecked her sister on the cheek and rushed from the house.

"Give our love to Bronagh, now. And ring me when you get there, you hear me?" shouted her sister.

"Aye, Sinead, I hear ye," her sister shouted back, laughing as she headed for the bus stop.

Sinead watched her departing sister until she was well out of sight. She hated the idea of Shauna going up to Belfast, but her niece was due to have her baby any day now and she needed her mother by her side. If Sinead hadn't been feeling under the weather she would have gone with her. Little was she to know that would be the last time she would ever see her sister.

* * * * *

The journey had been an uneventful one with Shauna dozing on and off. Travelling on the bus always did this to her. Mind you with the never-ending green of the countryside it was easy to nod off.

As they got closer to the border, the driver began to slow the bus down. There hadn't been any trouble lately but, it was always better to be safe than sorry. To him the bloody IRA could be anywhere, so he needed to be on the alert. Despite the overgrown hedgerows he still had a reasonably good view of the fields. Everything looked clear so he relaxed a little, although remaining alert just in case.

Looking ahead the driver could see the border crossing. The bloody British guards were patrolling back and forward. It didn't matter which side you supported, to him they were all rotten. The IRA and the British. They could all go to hell as far he was concerned. All he wanted was his Guinness and a peaceful life; that's all.

Suddenly a flash caught his eye. Swivelling his head he looked to the left, then gently braked. There was nothing. He was getting too old to be doing this run. Shaking his head, he decided his mind was beginning to play tricks on him. Placing his foot gently on the gas pedal he moved the bus forward, getting ready to approach the crossing barrier.

"Can everyone have your passports out and ready please," he called out.

They were the last words he ever said.

* * * * *

The gunfire had come from both sides of the

road. The two British guards at the barrier were quickly mown down. One of the bullets had hit the driver in the back, causing him to fall forward, his foot pressing hard on the gas pedal meaning the bus lurched forward. He had fallen across the steering wheel, and despite being dead, had turned the wheel sharply to the left, causing the bus to drive straight through the hedgerow into the river which ran alongside the road.

Screams could be heard from the passengers as they tried to dive for cover. But the machine gun fire coming from the reinforced British guards had not stopped, pouring into the area. The bullets had ploughed into the hedgerows, trees, woodlands, and the bus, killing any, and all caught up in the line of fire. The IRA had reciprocated, with their firing hitting the self-same targets in the same free abandonment, having no care for life or limb.

Fifteen minutes later silence reigned.

Bodies of the IRA and the British Soldiers lay across the road and in the fields. The bus was decimated. Holes ran along every side of it. Inside, bodies, or parts thereof, were strewn across the seats and the floor. The driver was practically shot to pieces. One had to pity the poor person trying to identify him afterward. As for Shauna, she lay in a pool of her own and her seat partner's blood. The man, a stranger, had tried his best to protect her from the hail of bullets. But such was the force from both sides that no one had stood a chance of survival. It was a black day in hell for both the British... and the IRA.

COLEEN

The aftermath...

News of the unprovoked attack was broadcast across the country and then worldwide. Condemnation of both the IRA and the British spread far and wide, but that would be no consolation to Shauna's family.

The first Coleen and her family heard of the ambush was later that evening. Having finished tea, Sinead had been wondering why her sister hadn't been in touch. Was there a problem with her niece? As her husband turned the TV on, there was the answer to her worries, staring out at her from the TV screen.

The shock was too much for Sinead to bear. Collapsing to the floor in grief, her husband had to ring for an ambulance. They quickly took his wife to the local hospital where the doctors announced she had suffered a severe heart attack. Little did they know she would never get over the shock of losing her sister.

As the weeks passed, Coleen thought her mother might survive. As the days passed she appeared to be improving. That was until the news came that her cousin, Shauna's daughter in Belfast had lost her baby.

The loss of her mother in the ambush had so deeply shocked the young mother it had caused her to have a premature birth. The baby had been a boy, but he had been still born. This additional upset was too much for her mother's weak heart. Upset at the loss of her beloved sister the news of her niece and the baby was too much. She relapsed, suffering another massive heart failure. The family, being too late to be at her bedside, were devastated.

* * * * *

The funeral was over. The sun had shone with the turnout of attendees being good. Looking at her father, Coleen realised that he had aged considerably in a matter of days. Gone was the fun-loving, smiling man he once was. Now he was just an empty shell of himself, sitting in his chair by the fireside, lost in his own thoughts. At night she often heard him crying. And although Coleen wanted to go and comfort him she knew he wouldn't welcome her interfering in his grief. There finally came a point where Coleen began to think she might have to speak to the doctor about him. But as time passed, slowly her father started to talk again. However, he would never really be the same happy man he had been when his wife was alive.

About three weeks after the funeral there was a knock at the door. When Coleen opened it she was surprised to find Mr. O' Connell standing on the doorstep. Having been brought up to be a polite child she automatically invited him to speak to her father.

O' Connell was the local IRA representative. Her father was not amused. In fact, he was downright bloody angry.

As the man started offering his condolences for the family's loss it was more than her father could bear. Controlling his temper, he finally said, "You've said ye piece, so I suggest you now leave."

Which would have been fine had the man not started spouting that the fight for freedom must go on. It was at this point that her father lost his temper, and taking O' Connell by the arm, he said, "Coleen, open the door."

Thereupon, he marched the man out into the street cursing him and all the IRA followers to boot. Coleen had never seen her father so angry; neither had Mr. O' Connell, and he had known him a lot longer than her. This was perhaps the turning point for her father.

COLEEN

Boat to safety...

After the visit of Mr. O'Connell, Coleen's father started giving serious thought to his daughters' safety. That meant she needed to be out of Ireland. And so, a couple of days later he contacted his sister who now lived in England, arranging for Coleen to go and stay with her until the troubles had either eased or were over.

Coleen knew little of her aunt other than she had left Ireland under a cloud. According to her cousin, her aunt had been pregnant and as the church didn't look kindly on unmarried mothers she had had no choice but to leave the country... fast. That lady now lived in Brampton where she worked in some element of the National Health Service to do with motherhood.

Although Coleen didn't want to leave her da' and her brother she knew better than to argue with him. And so, it was approximately three weeks later that Coleen packed her belongings and prepared to leave her beloved Ireland for God knew how long. This time both her father and her brother took her north to Dublin where she boarded a ship for England. It had been agreed that her aunt would meet her at the port when she landed.

Standing at the dock side, Coleen looked up at the ship she was about to board for her trip across the Irish Sea. "Do I have to go, Da'?" she asked.

Holding back his tears, her father said, "Yes." His reply was brusque and sharp. Pulling himself together he swallowed hard and said, "Sorry, Mavourneen. I just want you to be safe," and he took her in his arms to ease the tension.

Finally saying their goodbyes Coleen boarded the ferry that would take her away from her family. It was a tearful farewell, and she knew it would be some time before they were whole once more.

* * * * *

Arriving in Liverpool some eight hours later Coleen was both excited and nervous about staying in England. She had never been far from her home in Ireland, never mind to another country. And, if there was thing England was, it was certainly another country. Considering the time of year, the crossing had been relatively quiet for the Irish Sea but still, Coleen was thankful that this part of the journey was coming to a close.

Half an hour later Coleen took her first steps on British soil. Going through customs and passport control she finally walked through the doors into a large hall where the noise hit her. People were moving about and chatting, the high ceiling causing the noise to echo and vibrate all around. Nervously Coleen searched the number of people waiting to greet her fellow passengers and then, all at once, she saw her aunt waving.

"Coleen, Coleen," her aunt called, waving to her enthusiastically.

Waving back, Coleen breathed a sigh of relief. At last a familiar face. Her aunt looked just like her da' and suddenly felt as if she had come home.

FRANCIS
(KNOWN AS FRAN)

Following in other steps…

Fran had had what could be called a very normal upbringing. Well, at least she thought so. She was the only child of parents who had married later in life. Although a child had never actually been on the cards both parents were delighted when, at the ripe age of forty-two, her mother found herself pregnant. Up to that point both her parents had been wrapped up in their individual careers – her father being a barrister – her mother a county court judge. In fact, her mother was one of the youngest court judges there was on the circuit. Obviously, there had been some questions about professional conflict, but both her parents were sticklers for the rules so their ethics were never called into question.

With a young child on board, Fran's mother had decided to reduce her workload. However, with being a stay-at-home mother not the ideal for her, she had set up an agency allowing people, who couldn't afford to go down the normal route of a solicitor, to get legal advice at a subsidised cost. The agency had got some great support and finding from local government, proving to be such a great success it had developed into quite a successful concern. During her formative years, Fran had attended the office with her mother, being kept safely in her pram. However, once she was old enough to be left her mother, having found a well-qualified child-minder to look after her daughter, had returned to the bench part-time. As Fran grew older her mother had retaken up the position full-time, even sitting on some major cases.

During her early school years, Fran had attended private schools, mainly because her parents didn't want her mixing with the locals, some of whom were not the best behaved in the district. When not away at school Fran had, in essence, had a lonely childhood. With no siblings and few local friends, she had needed to find some way to occupy her mind.

When her Grandmother (her Father's mother) came to live with them she finally had someone to communicate with. Soon she began asking questions about her late Grandfather and over time she began to read about her late Grandfathers military history. Grandfather Thompson had been enrolled in the British army during the world war, quickly being promoted to Major and becoming a decorated war hero. He had, according to her Grandmother, been a daring fellow.

Fran was delighted to sit and talk to her

Grandmother as she loved talking about the tall, handsome, soldier in uniform that she had fallen in love with.

"It was love at first sight," she told Fran. "He was so good-looking. And all the other girls were jealous because he chose me to dance with him. And when he took me home later that night he kissed me," and she laughed girlishly. "Do you know, Fran, I had never been kissed before. Have you been kissed yet?"

Shuddering, Fran pulled a face of disgust. "Erg… Yuck, Gran, that's disgusting. Who would want to kiss a boy? They smell."

Her Grandmother had laughed, saying, "You will one day, Fran. When you meet the man you want to marry."

But Fran wasn't so sure. From what she'd seen of boys they were horrible. Mind you being only twelve years old how was she to know if all boys smelled. She had only met a few. Still, she had to agree with Gran, her Gramps had certainly been a good-looking chap when he was younger. And her Dad took after him. Maybe that was why her Mom had fallen for him, letting him kiss her.

'But look what happened after she did. She got me,' she thought.

* * * * *

At the age of thirteen, Fran moved schools,

joining the local Brampton Grammar School where she became part of the Brampton Musketeers. They were a good bunch of girls and for the first time in her life, Fran had some friends.

FRANCIS
(KNOWN AS FRAN)

A future planned...

It was only as she grew older, and through reading more about her Grandfather and his military heroism did it dawn on Fran how much she would like to be just like him. One day she had asked her Dad if they took girls into the army.

He had laughed, saying, "Probably? I don't know, Frannie. Why? Are you thinking of joining up," and he had laughed again as if the idea of his daughter becoming a squaddie was amusing.

Despite her father's response to her questions, Fran decided that she would, when old enough look into joining the forces. She knew her parents would prefer it if she followed them into law. But, to her that was boring and it didn't interest her. Yes, she needed to find out more.

* * * * *

By the time Fran reached the final year of school, she had made her mind up that she was definitely going to join the army. As it happened there was a military recruitment office on the high street of their town. So, one Saturday, Fran decided she would call in to see if girls were accepted into the forces.

Arriving at the office, Fran found it was situated in an old travel agent that had gone bust the previous summer. The building had stood empty for months, often being vandalised by the local yobs. But having been taken over by the military it had been done up, having a pull-down grill to make it secure at night.

Taking a deep breath, Fran slowly opened the door and looked inside.

"Come on in, young lady?"

Looking at the person who had spoken, Fran saw a tall man aged about forty years. He was dressed in a Sergeants uniform. "Come on, I don't bite," he said.

Entering, Fran continued to look around.

"So, tell me what can I do for you?" the soldier asked.

"Err… I was err… wondering. Err… do you accept girls?"

Smiling, the Sergeant said, "We most certainly do. The Queen's Military is an equal opportunity force. Which service do you fancy joining - Army, Navy, or Airforce?"

Surprised that she would have a choice, Fran returned his smile, saying proudly, "Oh, the army. My Gramps was in the army. He was a war hero. He's got lots of medals."

"Did he now? Well, let us have a look," and he sat at the computer placed on the desk. "So, what was his name?"

"Christopher Gerald Thompson. He was in Burma, I think?"

Tapping away at the keyboard, the Sergeant finally located details of Fran's late Grandfather. He started reading about him, then suddenly he let out a whistle. "Wow, he certainly was a hero. And he got lots of medals. Oh, and… he was mentioned in despatches… more than once. Well, young lady, it looks like you are going to have a hard act to follow. So, let's get some details from you and see what we can do about making you a hero, sorry heroine, as well."

Sitting down, Fran took the form offered by the Sergeant and started filling it in.

"You do realise, you will need your parent's permission to join up, don't you?"

Fran nodded. That was one fight she wasn't looking forward to. But, with her Gran backing her she was determined to get her way. Having completed the form she handed it back for the Sergeant to check it over. Happy that everything was okay, he returned it to her, instructing her that she would need to get her parents to sign it. Once they had she could return the form to him, he would then send it off to headquarters and get the ball rolling, so to speak. She would also have to send details of her school attendance and her final exam results when she left school. After which, if she had been accepted into the military training school, she would receive notice of when and where to go for her medical. Once she'd passed that she would be given further details of her training dates.

Standing, the Sergeant then gathered some pamphlets together before handing them to her so she would have something to read, and to show her parents that explained the full process. He then held out his hand.

Taking hold of his, she shook his hand. His grip was firm but not bone-crushingly so.

"I'll wish you all the luck, and I hope to see you back here for completion of your application as soon as you've finished school."

Thanking him Fran left the office.

As she walked down the street Fran appeared to have suddenly matured. Her walk was more like a march than a stroll and her back was ramrod straight. From behind the window, the Sergeant watched her walk away thinking that there was potential officer material.

As Fran had left the enrolment office she was smiling from ear to ear. She had made the most important decision of her life. She was going into the

Army. There was just one problem. How was she going to convince her parents to accept her career choice? It would be hard but she knew she would get them to agree, somehow.

Yet despite her concerns that they wouldn't agree, and their misgivings about her choice of career, Fran did get her way, leaving for the training academy some two months later. Much to the surprise of everyone she knew, including her fellow Musketeers.

ZHORA

Approaching womanhood…

The older Zhora got the more afraid she had become. Recently, she had started her periods. That meant she would now be classed as a woman. Which also meant her mother would start looking for a future husband for her. The thing was, Zhora did not want to get married. To her men were hopeless. They couldn't be trusted, especially if they turned out to be anything like her eldest brother, Rashid.

As far as she was concerned, her brother was pure evil. And she wasn't too sure about her younger brother, Saleem either.

And yet, Rashid hadn't always been untrustworthy, not in the early days. When they were growing up, Rashid, Saleem, and her had all got on extremely well. But, something had changed in him, turning him into something vile and horrible. Having no thought for anyone but himself. Yet, despite all that, their mother had continued to love and favour him. Regardless of his bad behaviour.

School was coming to a close soon, and Zhora was beginning to dread the approach of those last few weeks. The Musketeers were all trying to be supportive but they just didn't understand what her life was going to be like. Her mother had gone to Pakistan and was due back shortly, having informed her father she had found a good husband for their daughter, and a wife for Saleem their youngest son. Zhora still hated the idea of getting married and was tempted to plead with her father to say no to the offer. But she knew it wouldn't work, that he wouldn't listen to her. She was expected to marry, and marry she would.

Oh, he had been lenient with her so far, much more than her mother liked. He had let her have none-Asian friends. The Musketeers were a great bunch of girls, although she had never dared invite any of them to her home, Mainly because she knew her mother would have been horrible to them. But still, they had always been nice, accepting her into the netball team and spending class breaks with her.

But now it looked like a fete accompli. Her mother had found her a husband. Yuck. Her dreams of becoming a fashion designer would go up in smoke, as surely as night followed day. She wanted to scream with rage.

* * * * *

With her mother having now returned she had been doing the rounds, bragging to all the neighbours about the rich husband she had managed to snag for her only daughter. It was planned that he and his family would be visiting England very soon to approve and finalise the marriage. The happy couple would be wed in the local registry office before they all flew to Pakistan where the proper wedding would take place in front of all the family etc.

'Yuck,' thought Zhora. 'Happy couple, indeed. Her mother was delusional.'

"Please, Allah, save me from this wretch of a man my mother has lined up for me," she prayed out loud.

Unfortunately, no one answered, but little did Zhora know that her prayers had been heard.

ZHORA

Her prayers are answered...

It was about two weeks after her mother's return that all hell broke loose. A bomb had gone off in the local precinct causing untold damage and killing a total of thirty-seven people. Sadly, the casualties were mainly women and children who were out shopping ready for Christmas. The police announced that it was a terrorist attack.

Everyone was shocked. As people met they all asked the same questions; Why our area? Why our town? Who could have done such a horrific thing? As the people gathered together a cry for action came from all sections of the community. They wanted action and they were to get it.

Within two days the terrorist squad of the police force started rounding up suspects. People who had spoken out were quickly gathered together and marched away to the police cells. No one was exempt - including Zhora's family.

Answering the door, Zhora's father was shocked to discover four armed police officers wanting to know where Rashid, her brother, was. Asking why he was wanted, they were told he was a suspect in the bombing. Her father was shocked. And so was Zhora. She knew her brother was a nasty piece of work but planting a bomb? He couldn't be involved - could he?

Her father told the Officers Rashid wasn't in but they still insisted on coming inside and searching the house. The police searched their home from top to bottom. Fortunately, it was clean. Throughout, her mother continued to complain about police brutality, wrongful arrest, etc. Then when they started opening her drawers her mother began screaming that they had no right to go through her personal belongings.

Finally, after an officer told her to be quiet or she would be arrested she began harassing her husband. Telling him he was a coward, allowing the 'pig' to speak to her. On and on she went, until finally, Zhora turned around and told her to shut up as she was making it worse for the family. Her mother then began screaming at Zhora, calling her bad names, like slut, whore, and telling her she was ugly and worthless. Zhora was so shocked, she burst into tears.

Carrying on regardless, finally, her father turned around and told her mother, "Shut up, woman. This is your fault. You have spoilt him, bringing him up badly." Her mother looked at her father, shock spread across her face. But, instead of remaining quiet, she started to complain at him so he held his fist to her face threateningly, saying, "Shut up, or I will shut you up."

No one in the family had ever seen their father behave in such a way towards their mother before. Even the police officers were a little surprised, but they did not interfere. Their mother shut her mouth, sat down but then she started muttering under her breath until her husband looked at her and she finally got the message to remain quiet.

Once the police had left, their father had gone upstairs and packed Rashid's belongings. He had then taken them to his sons' friend's house, telling him to look after them. Next, he had helped Rashid's wife pack all hers and their children's belongings. He had rung his brother in Birmingham to come and collect her, explaining it would be better if she left the area. For her own safety, he had told her.

Three days later, Rashid was arrested. When he rang to ask his father for help, the man just put the phone down on him without speaking. Rashid got the message. He had wronged the family and would never be forgiven for his evil actions.

ZHORA

The best-laid plans…

A week later the phone rang. Slowly her father went to answer its summons. He had been expecting the newspapers again, but this time the call was different. Zhora arriving home from school caught the end of the conversation.

"Yes, I am afraid it is true…."

"Yes… We are all deeply saddened and ashamed by his behaviour. A great disappointment…"

"No… I understand… Yes, I will tell the family the news… Thank you for ringing. Khuda Hafiz – Goodbye," and he put the phone down.

After standing for a few seconds her father finally turned and looked at Zhora. Giving her a weak smile, he said, "I'm sorry, Bita, but there will be no marriage. The family has heard of Rashid's arrest. They have cancelled their offer."

Zhora smiled back. It was obvious to her father that his daughter was in no way broken-hearted at the decision.

"What," screamed her mother upon hearing the news. "How dare they? They cannot do that. I will not allow it. Rashid has done nothing wrong. He is my

67

child, I love him. I believe he is innocent."

Whether it was the stress of the last few weeks since Rashid's arrest or the long-standing behaviour of her mother, Zhora would never know. But, turning towards his wife, her father slapped her across the face. "Nothing wrong!" he shouted. "Nothing wrong! Oh, no! He's done nothing wrong, only helped to kill thirty-seven innocent people, that's all. You, woman, will from this moment keep your mouth shut. You will never, ever mention his name in this house ever again. And, I am warning you, here and now, if you open your mouth again then you can pack your case and go home to your mother," and he stopped himself from saying anything else.

Then moving towards the door, he must have changed his mind for he concluded, "I never want to look at your face again, woman. You brought that spawn of hell into this world. If you love him that much, go and join him, but I repeat, his name will not be spoken in this house again for as long as I live, do you understand me?" and leaving the room he slammed the door behind him.

From that day on her father never spoke another word to her mother, nor did he look at her. Even when on his death bed, a few months later, and she was begging him to forgive her, he would not look at her, he just told her, "You can go to hell with that evil spawn of a son."

As her father passed away he held his daughter's hand and before he passed he made Zhora promise to live her life the way she wanted to live it. She was not to be brow-beaten by her mother. Zhora promised with all her heart she would do as he asked and that she would make a success of her life.

Following her father's death, her mother took to her bed. Zhora wasn't sure what to do. Rashid had been charged with an act of terrorism and faced life imprisonment. This meant the family continued to live under a black cloud. With Saleem being the only son now, it was left to him to take charge but he was as useless, as Rashid had been evil.

In the end, it all came down to Zhora. She had managed to find a job. Luckily it was with a local seamstress and it would prove to be her saving grace.

ZHORA

A promise kept…

Having worked for the seamstress for a couple of years, Zhora was eventually able to offer dress designing services. Soon, the reputation of her ability to design clothes, as well as sew them, began to spread. Maggie, the lady who owned the business, was delighted, as it increased her customer base. With so much work, Maggie offered Zhora a better position with more money. It was this that had encouraged her to start saving. Up to now, she had given all her earnings to her brother towards the household expenses. But the extra money she decided was for her, so off to the post office, she went and opened a savings account. She would keep the savings book in a safe and secure place at the dress shop. Perhaps her dream of owning her own business was now a possibility. Or was it?

Two days later, around lunchtime, Ray Gordon walked into the dress shop. There was only Zhora on duty as everyone else had gone for lunch.

"Can I help you?" she asked.

Looking exceedingly embarrassed, he smiled. "Err… I'm wanting some costumes made. I don't suppose you do that sort of thing do you?"

"We can make anything. Who is it for?"

Smiling at her and laughing slightly, he said, "Well, actually, it's for me and my two mates."
The look on Zhora's face must have been one of shock as he went on, "We're not gay or anything. Not that there is anything wrong with being gay. No. It's just that we are doing a concert and are pretending to be a group of lady singers. It's for a charity event but, because we are all different sizes we can't get dresses to fit us all. So… I err… wondered if you could help. We'll pay you, we don't' expect them for nothing," and he stopped speaking looking slightly embarrassed.

Zhora thought for a moment. She liked the look of this young man. He was good-looking. She had never really looked at an English man before, but she liked what she saw. Finally, she said, "Well, yes, I can make the dresses. The cost would depend on the style and sizes – how much material and the time it takes to make each dress. It's a bit difficult unless I can get some measurements. When do you need them for?"

Relaxing, Ray smiled at her. "That's the trouble we need them two weeks on Saturday if that's possible."

Zhora nodded her head. She could do that if the dresses weren't too complicated. "Tell you what can you get the others together so I can take measurements. And, do you have any idea of style?"

Grinning Ray, said, "As I said, it's for a charity that helps children overseas. We're err... going to be singing a Beverley Sisters numbers. It's something for the oldies. You've probably never heard of them." As he said the words Ray suddenly blushed. "Oh! I'm so sorry, I shouldn't have said that."

Laughing, Zhora said, "That's okay. And you are right, I haven't heard of them. Okay, when can you pop in for me to take measurements?"

"Err... how about six o'clock this evening?" Agreeing that it would be a good time to call, Zhora said she would look the singers up online and come up with a dress design for them.

Ray thanked her, saying, "Thanks, that's great. See you at six. Bye. Oh, by the way, what do I call you, Miss?"

"Zhora. Just call me Zhora, bye."

* * * * *

At precisely six o'clock, the doorbell to the dress shop rang signalling the arrival of Ray and his two friends, Mark and Jack. As Zhora greeted them she realised Ray had been right about their different sizes. Ray was the tall, slender one, while Mark was more the cuddly type, and Jack was shorter than the other two.

"Okay, gentlemen, do I presume you haven't worn dresses before?" she asked. They all shook their heads. "That's okay. If you will take your jackets off, I can measure you and then show you a couple of styles that I think would suit all of you."

Half an hour later, having all agreed on the style of dress, Mark and Jack left the shop. After they had left, Ray said, "Err… Zhora, do you fancy a coffee? That is if it's okay for you to be seen out with me?"

Zhora smiled. She liked Ray, and whether her family agreed to it or not, she was going to go and have a coffee with him. What had her father told her? Enjoy yourself. So, to hell with what anyone thinks. Locking up the shop, they strolled down the street to the Blue Dream, coffee shop. An hour later, Zhora left for home. She had just spent the best hour of her life so far.

ZHORA

What's wrong with him?...

The romance with Ray developed, as did Zhoras post office bank account. She was, more than ever, determined now to achieve her goal. And she would, as long as her mother didn't try and throw a spanner in the works by talking about marriage. She wouldn't be surprised if her mother tried to do just that.

Ray and Zhora had started dating seriously, and recently he had declared that he loved her and wanted to marry her. She had been shocked. But, if she was honest she was also very happy.

* * * * *

Arriving home a few weeks later, Zhora was surprised to find her mother sitting on the settee. This in itself seemed suspicious. "Feeling better?" she asked.

Her mother ignored her. Zhora shrugged her shoulders and carried on with what she was doing. Finally, her mother spoke. "I have arranged a husband for you. He will be arriving from Pakistan next week to conclude the arrangements."

Zhora could not believe what she was hearing. Slowly turning to look at her mother, she took a deep breath, then carefully, she said, "Well, he is going to be very disappointed isn't he?"

Her mother sat up in the chair. "What is that supposed to mean?"

"It means that I do not wish to marry any man that you think I should. In fact, I have no intention of marrying any man you choose for me. So, you had better get back on the phone so you can tell him and his family he needn't bother coming, because I won't be here to greet him."

"You will do as I say," shouted her mother. "Or else."

"Or what, Mother? Have you told him we have a terrorist in the family? Ahh… I see from your face that you haven't. Well, believe you me, I will certainly tell him. And, if I don't, you can be damn sure the bloody neighbours will. Oh no, Mother, I will not marry any man you say, because your choice of men is as bad as your choice of sons to love. Absolute crap. Besides, my father made me promise to live my life my way and that is what I am going to do. And if you don't like my response, well I honestly don't give a damn." Then turning Zhora picked up her bag and left the house. There was only one place she could go.

To see Ray.

* * * * *

Half an hour later, Zhora knocked on Ray's

door. As soon as he opened the door and saw her standing there he knew something was wrong. She was shivering and had obviously been crying. Taking hold of her hand he gently led her indoors.

"Tell me what's wrong, sweetheart."

Before she could respond, Zhora had burst into tears again and was sobbing hard. Leading her into the lounge he sat her down, waiting until she had calmed down. Once she had, Zhora explained what had happened at home, telling him she had just walked out. She also told him about Rashid and him being in prison. About her father being dead, and how it was all her mother's fault. The floodgates just opened. By the time she had finished Ray knew everything about her.

"So, sweetheart, what would you like to do? You know I want to marry you," he said.

Looking at him, she asked, "Even though you know about Rashid?"

Smiling, he said, "I don't want to marry Rashid, I want to marry you. Do you want to stay here? Or shall I put you into a hotel?"

It was at this point that Zhora knew she had found the right man for her. He could just have taken advantage of her but no, he was thinking about her all the time. Slowly she said, "I just want to stay here. With you," and leaning forward she kissed him.

* * * * *

Ray and Zhora were married ten days later at the local registry office. Mark and Jack agreed to be witnesses. Zhora had worried over what her family would say or do. After all, there had been many cases of honour killings so she was frightened of their reaction. To ease her mind, Ray, in his position as a lawyer, wrote a letter informing her family that Zhora had left home, and that she was now married. He also told them that it was now a matter of legal record, and if anything happened to her the police would be informed that they were responsible for it. He also raised an injunction that would prevent her family from communicating with her for the next six months. These were strong measures but he understood fully

Over time Zhora and her family reached a tentative agreement and the family relationship recommenced. However, Ray would often remind them that if anything happened to his wife he would bring the full force of the law down on their heads. Despite her not liking her new son-in-law, Zhoras mother had to accept that in this instance she had lost the battle.

LORRAINE

The air-head rules...

"Lorraine! Sit up and shut up," demanded the teacher.

All eyes in the class turned to stare at Lorraine who had been busy chatting away to Teddy Smith. They were two air-heads together, often being pulled up by the class teacher for disrupting lessons. This was the third time he had called her name out. It seemed Lorraine just couldn't help it – she just loved to talk.

Crossing the room the teacher stood in front of Lorraine's desk. Placing his hands on top of the desk he looked her in the eyes, calming telling her, "If you speak one more time I'm going to send you to the Head. Do you understand? Well, do you?"

Lorraine nodded, saying nothing. "I'm waiting, Lorraine, what do you say?"

"You said I couldn't talk anymore, Mr. Walker. If I answer you then I'm talking, aren't I?"

The whole class cheered. Annoyed at being caught out, Mr. Walker shouted, "Be quiet, or you will all get detention."

As peace reigned in the room once more, Mr. Walker shouted, "Get on with your work, all of you." However, walking back to his desk he let a slight smile cross his face. Lorraine was quick, having got one over on him this time.

* * * * *

"So, what do you want to do when you leave school?" Coleen asked as the Musketeers sat chatting, waiting for the schools' careers officer to arrive.

Zhora said, "I'm going to go into dress design. I want my own business. What about you, Loly?"

Lorraine looked up and grinning, she said, "I'm going to join the police force."

The room was silent. No one spoke. Had they just heard correctly? The blonde-haired, air-head that was Lorraine, the one who was always disrupting the class, keeping them all in stitches, wanted to join the police. All at once, the whole room burst out laughing.

"What the hell, Loly," Ted called out. "They won't have you in there. You never stop talking," and they all burst out laughing again.

Trying to look indignant and not laugh either, Lorraine, said, "I will have you know, Ted Smith, that I will make a damn good police officer. And when I do, you lot had better watch out, 'cause I won't hesitate to nick you if I have to," and despite her best intentions not too, she burst out laughing.

Little did any of them realise exactly what Lorraine was capable of.

About a month after they had left school,

Lorraine met up with Fran for a coffee. "So, when do you leave for training camp, Fran?"

"Next week. I'm excited and frightened at the same time. I think my parents aren't too happy about it but at least they have finally accepted my decision and are trying to be supportive. What about you, Lol?"

Lorraine smiled, nodding her head, as she understood the thing about parents. "Another two weeks and I'm off. Can't wait. I'll be glad to get away from here. Dad has been giving me lots of earache. I don't think he likes it that he's going to have a copper in the family," and she laughed gleefully.

Fran joined in. "I have to say, I think all the class was a bit surprised about your choice of career but hey, great on ya, Lol. I've joined the army because my Gramps was a war hero. Do you think we'll do okay? You know… us being… girls!"

"We sure will, Fran. Remember, we're part of the Musketeers. All for one…" said Lorraine.

"And one for all," finished Fran.

* * * * *

Three months later, Lorraine graduated from the police academy, having completed her basic police training. Despite her Dad's reluctance, both her parents were, in the end, proud of what their daughter had achieved. It was strange how she had gone from being the class air-head, who never stopped talking, to graduating top of her class at the academy. And though it would take her a further three years to complete her full training she would always come out top of her class every time.

What Lorraine hadn't shared with the Brampton Musketeers was her ultimate goal. She desired to achieve success in her chosen career. And that success meant becoming a Chief Inspector of Police. Over her time in the force, she would make sure she reached and achieved that role successfully.

LORRAINE

Success smiles down…

Lorraine had been in the job almost fifteen years when she met Mark, her fiancée. Oh! She'd had a few romances, but usually short-lived ones. Most hadn't lasted long as she was moved from area to area, and then county to county. Some of her relationships had been purely sexual.

There had been Jock, up in Edinburgh. She had met him when called to give evidence in court. He was an Immigration Lawyer representing a company that had been employing some illegal workers. Lorraine had been part of the team involved in the surveillance of the company. When the team had crashed into the building they had discovered the owner tied up. The illegals had robbed him, making off with one of his vehicles and the cash from the safe. The matter had become complicated after that.

Anyway, Jock had asked her out for dinner at the end of the case. He had a nice smile and a good chat-up line so she had agreed. They had dated for some eight months. Lorraine always thought the sex had been great. That was until she discovered he had been in the 'closet' for ten years, only deciding that last year together to come out. It appeared, gay lawyers were being accepted as the norm. They broke up not long afterward. Sad really as they had got on very well.

Moving on to Glasgow, Lorraine had then had a fling with a fellow officer called Alasdair – Al for short. He had been a plain-clothes detective, but he liked his scotch too much. One night, having drunk too much, he had lashed out at her, so Lorraine had floored him. When he came round, she had gathered up her stuff and gone home, refusing to speak to him again until he got help.

The last she knew of him he had been kicked off the force for being drunk on duty and for nearly beating a criminal to death. The desk sergeant had thrown Al in a cell to sleep it off and called the on-duty doc to look at the injured man. It was the doctor who had raised the alarm, bringing a complaint against Al. It was not one of the Glasgow Police's finest hours.

There had been many other dalliances throughout her career. But, finally, being stationed in the county where her hometown of Brampton was situated, she was given a promotion to a higher rank.

* * * * *

Her progression up the ranks to Chief Inspector had been a steady one. It was while stationed in Brampton that she had met Mark. He had charmed her. Not being in the police force, Mark was involved in the theatre. He was also ten years younger than her. But there had been something about him that had drawn them together. He liked older, strong women who would boss him around, and she? What the hell had she seen in him?

Well, he was good-looking, charming, could talk the talk, and boy was he good in bed.

Although Mark could be away for weeks on end, travelling with various shows, when he was home it was great. He would cook, clean the house, and even have run a hot bath ready for her the moment she walked through the door. He would massage her back and shoulders, then they would make mad passionate love. It was a wonderful relationship. If he was performing locally, Lori would go and watch him perform. She had to admit, he was damn good on stage as well.

Being tall, good-looking, and slim, Mark always seemed to get the hero parts. This meant him kissing a lot of heroines. When Lori, first saw this happening she had been as jealous as hell, telling him so. Telling him she wouldn't come and watch him again. He had spent the night convincing her she was the only woman he loved. Also, when he kissed these other women, all he could think of was her. She had believed him. It might have been better if she hadn't.

* * * * *

They had been dating about twelve months when Mark moved in with her. She had a small apartment, which had been cosy enough for the odd night's stay over but was really too small for them living together full time. It was about this time that her Grandmother passed away, leaving Lorraine a large house and a small inheritance. As it happened Lori loved her Grans house so she decided that they would move into that. Although Mark went with her, Lorraine did wonder if perhaps he was not one hundred percent happy about the move. Anyway, they soon settled down to a nice home life.

Another eighteen months passed, and although Mark was as busy as ever travelling, this time often going abroad, he was still attentive when home. It was about this time that Lorraine decided she would like some companionship. Mark had suggested a dog but Lori knew she wouldn't always be available to walk a dog. Besides, with Mark away so much, he wasn't able to look after a dog either. Finally, they settled on a Blue Persian cat.

"At least cats can look after themselves, better than dogs," Mark had said. As it turned out Lorraine had agreed. And so 'Blue' had joined the family.

It was also around this time that Mark proposed. Up to this point, Lorraine had never thought about marriage. She was if she were truthful, quite happy just living together. Getting married would change the game. After giving the matter some thought, and with some charming talk from Mark, Lorraine finally succumbed and the pair announced their engagement.

Mark organised a party at the house one Saturday, which went with a swing. Everything seemed to be going great.

* * * * *

Mark and Lorraine had been engaged for nearly fourteen months and at first, both had enjoyed their new relationship. However, in recent months things had begun to change. It took Lorraine a long time to notice that it was the little things that she had missed.

Such as Mark not always answering the phone straight away when she knew he was at home. Or, him forgetting to collect her uniform from the dry cleaners, even after promising to do so. Sometimes not getting home until after her, with his excuse being he had been stuck at rehearsals.

There were other things which she also missed, such as him hiding his phone. Deleting text messages as soon as had received them. The lack of warmth in him. And the reduction in their sex life. His excuse often was that he was tired from all the travelling. When she suggested he slow down, as she earned enough for them anyway, he blasted her, causing a big row. Arguing was something, up until recently, they had never done. Lori began to get worried.

Unfortunately, due to the increase in the pressure of her new position, Lorraine would miss so much more.

SUSIE

Growing up…

The woman sat in the car waiting for her daughter to come out of school. Why her husband had insisted on their daughter going to this school she would never know. Why couldn't Susanne have gone to the private school she had chosen for her. But no, her husband had said it would do her good to mix with the local kids. She was not a happy woman.

"Hi, Mom," said Susie as she opened the car door. "Can we give Zhora a lift into town, please?"

About to say no, her mother nodded her head instead.

'Really,' she thought, 'what was her daughter doing mixing with the likes of this girl.'

Stopping at the shopping mall on the edge of town, Zhora, climbed out of the Mercedes car, politely saying, "Thank you for the lift. See you tomorrow, Susie," before she closed the door.

"Doesn't she know your name is Susanne," said her mother frigidly.

Looking at her mom, Susie raised her eyes in frustration. "Yea, of course, she does but we all have nick names. Mines' Susie. I like it. And… dad likes it too."

Her mother didn't speak. There were times when she hated her husband. It didn't matter what she said, where their daughter was concerned, if daddy said this, then it was okay. But, if she said anything then it was ignored.

Arriving home, Susie dashed from the car. She knew her mother didn't like her going to the school her dad had chosen – well, actually she had chosen it. It was strange how she could get anything she wanted from her dad. It all came down to her being daddy's little girl. Not that he overly spoiled her but he was super soft with her, letting her have most things. Susie was quite switched on, quickly learning just how far she could push her dad but always being careful in what she asked for.

Entering the hall, she called out, "Hi, Dad, we're home."

He responded with, "Hello, sweetheart, had a good day at school?"

Going to stand in his office doorway, she said, "Yes. We won the netball game again. We're getting good. You should come and see us play sometime. We need all the cheering on we can get."

Looking up at his daughter, he smiled, she was developing into a lovely young lady. He knew he would be jealous of the man who would eventually steal her heart from him. Smiling, he said, "If I'm not working I will. Now, I suppose, considering that you've won, you should be rewarded, shouldn't you?" and reaching into his pocket he withdrew a five-pound note. Offering it to her, he said, "Here, buy your teammates some treats for winning the game."

Taking the money she went forward and kissed her father on the cheek. Then turning she left the room, rushing upstairs to her bedroom so she could have a shower and get changed ready for their evening meal.

* * * * *

It wasn't so much that Susie was spoilt but more that it was her father's way of showing his love for her. His time was scarce, so money was the next best thing he could give her. Whether Susie knew she was being neglected or not, she never told anyone. But she wasn't the only one, as her mother had the same problem. While she wanted to get close to her daughter, unfortunately, she didn't know how. Maybe because she was always acting too posh for Susie, instead of behaving like a loving mom. This was very much a family at odds with one another.

Dinner was the only time the three members of the family actually spent some time together. But even that wasn't all the time, as on many occasions it was just Susie and her mother. At these times her father would stay in his office, having his dinner sent in on a tray. Still, when Susie and her mother did spend time together neither rarely spoke to one another. It was more that her mother didn't know what to say than that Susie had nothing to tell her. She didn't speak as she felt her mother just wasn't interested in her or in what she did each day.

There was, however, one taboo subject they never talked about - her older brother, Justin. He had left home nearly two years ago, after a big row with her mother. At the time Susie hadn't known why he had gone and hadn't heard from him again. That was until recently. And only then by accident.

She had been in town waiting for her mother to collect her when someone had said, "Suz? Susanne is that you?" Looking up, Susie was surprised. No one ever addressed her by her full name other than her parents.

At first, she hadn't recognised him. Then it hit her who it was. "Justin," she yelled, throwing herself into his open arms. "Where have you been? Why didn't you tell us you were coming home?"

Justin slowly stood away from her, looking a little sheepish. "Erm… I'm not coming home, Suz. I'm not welcome."

She couldn't understand his response, saying, "Of course, you'll be welcome," but the look on his face was sad. He shook his head no. "But why not?" She just didn't understand.

Sitting on the bench next to her, he said, "It's hard to explain, Suz. They... well, she, kicked me out."

"What, no never, Dad wouldn't do that. There must be some mistake."

"Sorry, Suz, no, there isn't. Look, I've been watching you for the last couple of weeks. Plucking up the courage to talk to you." He looked at his watch. "I know mom will be here soon to collect you. Can we meet next Saturday? What time can you get into town? We'll go somewhere for lunch or a coffee. Here is my phone number. Don't give it to anyone, please. Let this be our secret? I'll explain it all when I see you next week. Okay, sweetie? Loves ya," and before she could say anything he was gone.

As she sat looking at the piece of paper, she heard a car horn. Her mother had arrived and was letting her know it. Putting the piece of paper in the pocket of her jeans, she picked up her bag and dashed to the car.

"What took you so long?" her mother asked.

"Sorry. I was miles away. Got thinking about Justin."

"What. What about Justin? What on earth were you thinking about him for?" her mother asked, sounding slightly annoyed.

"Nothing really," said Susie, covering her

tracks. "I thought I saw him because I saw someone who just reminded me of him. I miss him that's all. He is my brother after all you know."

"Yes, well, he's no good. So good riddens to bad rubbish," her mother snarled, before turning the sound on the radio up, thus preventing any further talk on the subject.

That evening, as they sat at the dining table, Susie steered the conversation round to her having seen someone who reminded her of Justin. "Why did he go, dad? I do miss him you know?"

Her father didn't answer straight away but he looked across the table at his wife. It was not a nice look. "Who can say, sweetie. But, I miss him too, Suz," he said, after which he too changed the subject.

Susie was left wondering what it was Justin had done that had caused both her parents to not want to talk about her brother. 'Oh, well,' she thought. 'I'll find out next week when I see him.'

SUSIE

The truth…

The following Saturday, Susie's mother dropped her off in town, telling her to get the bus home as she might not have finished her dress fitting in time. This was good news for Susie as it meant she could meet up with her brother and spend all afternoon with him. As long as she caught the five o'clock bus home she would be okay.

Waiting until her mother had driven away, Susie set off for the shopping mall where she had planned on meeting Justin. Seeing her coming towards him, he waved. "Hi, Suz. What did the old bat say?" he asked.

She was a little surprised at the name he had called their mother, but would later understand why. Finding a cosy coffee shop where they could get a bite to eat, they ordered their food and drink, which Justin paid for. Then they found a table in the corner where they could chat quietly together.

"So, Justy! What's the big secret? And where have you been? Why can't you come home?" Susie jumped in with her questions before her brother had a chance to speak.

Swallowing the mouthful of food he was

chewing, Justin took a small drink of his coffee and sighed. "It's like this, Suz. Mom kicked me out, because... because I'm seeing someone."

Susie looked at him. "So? What's wrong with that? Is she nice?" Her brother didn't answer. As Susie went on, "Oh! I get it, she's not posh enough for mother. Is that it? Not good enough for her blue-eyed baby boy!" and she mimicked her mother's voice as she said it. She sounded so true to the real thing that Justin laughed; he couldn't help himself.

"Hell, kiddo, where did you learn to talk like her? If I was blindfolded I would almost believe it was her," and he laughed some more.

Laughing, Susie said, "When you've listened to her as much as I have it becomes easy to mimic her voice. So, what's she like then?"

Now it had come time to tell Susie the truth, Justin hesitated. He wasn't sure how she would react. In a low voice, he said, "It's not a girl, Suz. I'm dating... another... man. I'm... gay. You do know what that means don't you?"

Susie couldn't speak for a moment. Justin had left home because he was gay? No, it can't be true. "Are you sure," she whispered.

Laughing slightly, Justin looked at his sister, before saying, "Yes, sweetie. I'm sure. I've been dating Chris for nearly two years. We're engaged, and we're going to get married. I came to find you to see if you'd like to come to the wedding?"

Susie didn't speak. She wasn't quite sure what to say. After a long silence, she looked at her brother and said, "Does dad know?"

Justin nodded his head.

"Does he not like you being... you know... gay?"

"I'm not sure. He didn't stop mom kicking me out of the house, did he?"

"But dad misses you. He said so, only last week, that he misses you very much. He should have stopped her. She had no right sending you away. It's not fair."

Justin smiled at his sister. He loved her very much and knew the bond that had been forged the day she was born, still existed, and was as strong as ever. "Life isn't always fair, sweetie. But, I'm happy. Would you like to meet Chris?"

"Is he nice?" She had asked the question automatically, knowing full well if her brother liked... no loved this Chris, then he must be nice. "Yes, I would like to meet him," she told Justin.

Pleased, Justin said, "Well, if you eat up, I'll take you to the place where we live and introduce you."

* * * * *

As Susie rode home on the bus, in her mind she went over her meeting with Justin. Her brother looked

97

happy. Meeting his fiancée had seemed a little strange at first, but Chris had turned out to be as nice as Justin said he was. The afternoon had been full of laughter. When Chris had asked her if she would be a bridesmaid at their wedding she had eagerly said yes, being delighted as she had never, ever been a bridesmaid before.

The question which worried her most was whether or not to tell her parents – well not her mum maybe her dad at least. Arriving home she was still unsure what to do. As she closed the door to the house she called out, "Hi, Dad. I'm back."

Her father appeared at his office door. "Had a good day, sweetie?"

"Err… yes. Is mum home?" When her father shook his head no, she said, "Dad, can I talk to you, please?"

Furrowing his brow he wondered what had happened. Not wanting to panic he tried to appear casual, saying, "Of course. Come on into the study." Once inside, he said, "Okay, sweetie, what's the problem?"

Not sure where to start, Susie was left with only one option but to blurt out what she wanted to know. "Dad, is it true you kicked our Justin out because he's gay and is in love with another man?"

To say her father was floored was an

understatement. This had been the last thing he had expected to ever hear coming from his daughter's mouth. Without speaking he stood up, and going to the door he checked to see if his wife was about, then carefully he closed it shut, before returning to his chair. Once settled he finally managed to speak.

"No, Susie, I did not kick Justin out because he was gay. I have regretted the day your brother left, and wish he could come home. But it's not possible."

"Why not?" she demanded harshly. "He's done nothing wrong, has he?"

Her father looked at her, realising that his little girl was no longer that little. And while this was a conversation he had never wanted to have with her, much like not talking about periods and pregnancy, he knew he had to man up and face the fact that she was entitled to know the truth. Taking a deep breath he began. "Your mother discovered that Justin was dating some black guy."

"His name is Chris, and he's very nice."

"What. You've met him? When?"

Susie swallowed, and looking a little frightened, said, "Today. I met up with Justin and Chris today. They want me to be a bridesmaid at their wedding…" and her voice trailed off in a whisper.

Surprised, her father didn't respond at first. Eventually, he asked, "How is Justin? Does he look good?"

Smiling, Susie answered eagerly, "Oh, yes! He looks good. They've just come back from a holiday in Jamaica and he is nice and brown. They went to visit Chris's family. And they had a really good time. Justin says Chris's family welcomed him with open arms."

Her father suddenly realised this was probably the closest she would get at having a go at him without hurting him. Yet little did she know just how much it did in fact wound him. "Do you think Justin would like to come home?"

Susie thought for a moment. "Yes and no. He's missed me, and you, Dad. I don't think he will forgive mum. He might meet you if you ask him."

"Do you think so, sweetie? I'd like that. I need to say sorry to him."

"Why don't we ask him, dad? Make it our secret."

Father and daughter looked at each other and smiled. 'Why not,' thought her father. 'Time to take back control of his household. And if his wife doesn't like it, well… she'll soon learn to lump it, or else.'

"Do you know Suz, I would love to meet up with him. Can you arrange it?"

Nodding her agreement, daughter and father knew they now shared a wonderful secret.

SUSIE

A truce is called...

Three weeks later Susie and her father attended the local registry office. Susie's father had bought her a new dress for the occasion which they had kept hidden in a drawer in his office. His wife never ventured into the office so it was a well-kept secret. That particular day his wife was due to attend a special meeting of some women's group, so she had left the house early, which left plenty of time for father and daughter to dress for the wedding.

The event went off well, with Justin and his father reuniting. His father also welcomed Chris into the family, hugging him as warmly as he did his son. After the ceremony, at which Justin's father and Chris's mother were witnesses, they all went for lunch at a posh restaurant where their father insisted on paying the bill.

"It's a wedding gift, boys," he said. He hadn't felt this relaxed or as happy in a long time.

Leaving the restaurant after a lovely meal, Susie and her dad were saying goodbye to the newlyweds when her mother turned the corner and saw them. She couldn't believe what she was seeing. Her husband

and daughter were laughing, smiling, and hugging, a Jamaican man and woman. And in public. Without thinking she raced across the paved square, demanding to know what was going on.

"Oh! Hi mother. I'd like you to meet…" started Justin but he was cut off as she rounded on her husband.

"How dare you? Just what the hell do you think you're doing. And with my daughter too," she demanded.

Susie was suddenly afraid. It was obvious her mother was very angry and quite ready to cause a scene in public. Something she would normally never, ever do.

It was at this point that her father held his hand up as if to stop the vitriol that was ready to flow. Looking his wife straight in the eye, and in a low and calm voice, he said, "I am congratulating **our** son, and **his husband**, on **their** wedding day. **Our** daughter and **I** have just spent a most enjoyable morning and afternoon watching the **son I love,** marry the person **he loves**!   We then went and had a very tasty lunch with this young man's delightful mother, who is as happy as I am, that our two sons have found each other. **And**, if you don't like that, well in the words of Rhett Butler from Gone with the Wind, '*Frankly my dear, I honestly, don't give a damn*.'"

102

Having said all that, he turned his back on his wife and taking hold of his daughter's hand, he said, "Come on, Suz, I think you made a wonderful bridesmaid and deserve a gift for doing it so well. What would you like, sweetie? You too, boys. I haven't bought you a wedding gift yet, so let's go shopping. After all, nothing is waiting to welcome me at home!" Then turning towards the shopping mall he started to leave, trailing Susie behind him, with Justin, Chris, and his mother following, all with looks of sheer amazement on their faces.

No one said anything, they just followed. To both Justin and Susie, this was a side of their father they had never seen before. He had stood up to their mother at last. Something he hadn't done in a very long time.

Susie knew that life at home would never be the same. Oh, she would still get what she wanted from her dad, although Susie would never push too hard for stuff. Her mother would become more docile. Justin and Chris would visit them often. Although, when they did, her mother would usually manage to be out, or she would retire to her room. Not that any of them were that bothered as they still had fun without her presence.

Whether this bothered her mother or not, Susie didn't couldn't tell, and to be honest she wasn't actually bothered. What it did do was bring her father more alive. He started spending less time in his office and more time with Susie as he had become aware that she was growing up fast. He knew that soon some handsome young man would come along and sweep her off her feet and he would lose his little girl forever.

What he didn't tell Susie, was that the day she finally left home he had plans of his own. Plans that did not include his stuck-up wife; but for now that was his secret. However, in the meantime, he had suddenly found a new interest, becoming a regular attendee often being found in the audience cheering the Brampton Musketeers and the Brampton School Netball Team on. Susie was delighted.

THE PRESENT

Sometimes, one cannot control what happens in our life, so we tend to go with the flow, often because it seems such a good idea. But is it. Eventually, we start to question why we did or did not do those certain things. Why we chose to marry that particular person but not the other one? Why we chose to walk away from that place, that job, that life we wanted or were offered? And sometimes we regret those decisions we made. Yet we often live with the decisions we make regardless of the regrets.

The years have flown by. And despite their ups and downs, the Brampton Musketeers have lived their lives to the best of their ability. Each has tried to follow their chosen path in life. To achieve their goal.

Yet, what were all those plans they talked about during those last weeks of school when deciding what their future should be. They lived through the halcyon years of those school days where the seven forged their friendship; cemented at an early and impressionable age. Oh, for the joy of those lost school years.

But now, like us, they go forward.

And like us, for the Brampton seven, there will come a day, sometime in their lives, when they will find themselves at a point where there are important decisions that need to be made. There will be a crossroads in front of them with a choice of paths down which to walk. With each path leading to a different place where each can and will have a differing effect upon their future.

All we can do is hope that each of them will achieve their ultimate goals and find the happiness they long for. The question is have they achieved what they set out to do.

MELINDA

A new beginning...

"Will that be all, Madam," enquired her assistant from the lounge doorway?

Melinda didn't respond immediately so engrossed was she with the view from her apartment window. Her assistant waited, then coughed gently in an attempt to attract her employer's attention, causing Melinda to finally turn from the window.

"I'm sorry, Mary," she responded. "Yes. That will be all for today. We can finish the rest tomorrow. Go home and see that lovely husband of yours," and she smiled at her assistant who responded likewise.

As the lounge door closed Melinda returned to her perusal of the view from the window. She had moved into the apartment a few days ago. It wasn't out of necessity that she'd decided to relocate, but because she found she could no longer live in the large house on the other side of the city. The house held too many memories of her late husband. Apart from being too large for just one person, it had never really been hers, being filled with all the things Simon's late wife had purchased. Her husband had told her to change anything in the house she wanted to, but Melinda had never had the heart to do so, knowing a lot of the items held precious memories for him. She wasn't jealous of those feelings. They were in the past. She was his future. He loved her, otherwise, she would not have married him.

Simon had passed away just under six months ago. They had been married less than twelve months, although they'd lived together for the past fifteen years. Marriage had never really been on the cards for Melinda, as her independence had always been important to her. Moving into the apartment felt strange but she was glad about her decision to do so. The only problem had been the number of belongings she had had to go through before everything was completed. Luckily, the estate agent, with Mary's help, had taken over the disposal of much of the furniture, whilst the solicitor had handled the paperwork and the Will. That had finally left her with only her personal stuff. Having originally been packed away in boxes, moving meant she had to sort it out. And so, she and Mary had spent the last couple of days going through them. Now there was just one box left. The one that contained mementoes from her earlier life.

Pouring a small glass of sherry, Melinda sat on the settee and opened the box. Lifting out the Old Brampton School Year Book, Melinda quickly drew in a short breath. Flicking through the pages she stopped at the picture of the Netball team and smiled.

There had been seven of them on the team. The same team throughout the whole of their school years. They had become known as the 'Musketeers.'

Looking at the photo she remembered the day it had been taken. How happy they had been back then. Later that week, the team had gone on to play the last match of the season; the inter-school competition. Suddenly the memories of that last game came flooding back...

MELINDA

Memories…

"Come on Brampton," cheered the crowd from the side of the pitch. "Pass the ball."

Phillipa had the ball. She passed it to Melinda who sent it on towards Coleen. All three girls ran down the pitch as fast as they could. They only needed to get the next net to stop the other team from scoring and they would win. Coleen tossed the ball towards Phillipa but a member of the opposing team intercepted, snatching it mid-air. A loud noise went up from the opposing fans. Spurred on, the girl with the ball set off towards Brampton's net, aiming at scoring. But, just as she passed to a fellow team member, Zhora jumped up as high as she could.

Catching the ball mid-air she quickly threw it as hard as possible towards Susie. She in turn sent the ball on towards Fran who passed it on to Melinda, having found a chink in the opposing defence. Snatching the ball, Melinda bent and with an enormous jump, she lobbed the ball towards the net.

Everyone held their breath, watching closely as the ball floated across the court. It seemed to hover above the post for seconds, before slowly dropping then circling the top of the ring.

Would it fall in, or tip over the outer edge?

The seconds lingered on, no one dared to breathe, and then, just as the ref was about to blow her whistle the ball fell to the ground. Straight through the middle of the ring. Old Brampton had scored. The cheer went up. The crowd went wild with joyous relief and the girls in the team hugged each other. They had won.

'What a day that had been,' thought Melinda smiling. And how proud she had felt as their team captain.

* * * * *

A knock at the door heralded the arrival of her butler.

"My apologies, Madam. Mrs. Green has left some post for you. It was marked personal. I am sorry for not bringing it in before now."

Looking up, Melinda responded, "That's all right, Sims. We've all been rather busy today. Have you and Mrs. Sims settled in? I trust you are both satisfied with your quarters and will be comfortable?"

"Oh yes, Madam. We are more than satisfied and I'm sure we will be very comfortable. Shall I serve dinner at the usual time?"

Melinda agreed to the butler's suggestion, before taking the proffered mail from him.

After he had left the room, she looked at the name on the pink envelope, surprised to notice it was addressed to Miss. P Hammond – her maiden name. The address had been crossed out and others were written in their place a number of times. It had taken a long time to reach her. Of course, her father wouldn't send it directly to her as he had given up speaking to Melinda some years ago. She presumed her older brother must have forwarded it on.

Tearing the envelope open, she read the enclosed card. "A Reunion!" Melinda read out loud. Then she re-read the details again. Class of '64 Reunion! Everyone is welcome, including partners.

Looking at the card Melinda read that the organiser, and RSVP contact, was one Susie Smith nee Johnston. Melinda remembered Susie, thinking that she had been a bit of a show-off; always talking about what she'd done or what she had been bought. Susie's parents had been well off and could afford to buy her things. She, on the other hand, had had a poor upbringing!

Melinda suddenly felt guilty. It wasn't Susie's fault she had been spoilt, being the youngest child of elderly parents. Besides, Susie had been one of the Musketeers and they had all got on so well together.

Then Melinda remembered how Susie had always shared her sweets with her. Often giving

Melinda all of them, saying she was too full to eat anymore.

'It was because she knew I didn't get any sweets at home,' thought Melinda. 'Oh, what a bitch I am for thinking such unkind thoughts.'

Then she remembered how Susie had been so confident, so sure of what she wanted to do and what her life was going to be like once she left school. She had told everyone she was going to be a model and travel the world.

'Daddy will pay for me to go anywhere I want,' Susie would often say. Not realising that she was bragging. To her, that was what Daddy's did for their daughters.

Melinda wondered if Daddy had ever done any of that. 'Most probably,' she thought. After all, he'd been a wealthy businessman. And Susie's Mom had been very posh. Of course, the one disappointment was that her only daughter had been kicked out of private school, and ended up attending the local comprehensive.

"It seems that Daddy didn't have enough money to fix that little problem," Melinda spoke out loud.

Looking at the card again more memories came flooding back. 'Class of '64!' she thought with a smile.

The class had been a bit of a mixed bunch. Tommy Richards had got arrested a few weeks before the end of term. The Police had turned up at the school gates one day and carted him off to the local nick. He was later charged with six counts of burglary. He never did come back to school. Melinda smiled as she remembered how she'd had a crush on Tommy.

'Mind you,' she thought, 'he had been the best-looking boy in her school year. In fact, most of the girls had had a crush on Tommy. Him or Teddy (Edward) Smith.'

Melinda looked at the RSVP name again – Susie Smith (nee Johnston) it said. Could it be the same name? Surely not! Besides which, Susie's Mother would never have let her daughter go within a mile of the likes of Teddy Smith; especially if she thought they would ever get together.

"You are invited to the reunion of the Class of '64," she read out loud.

'No, no, I can't go,' she thought. She would feel awkward; the odd one out. Besides, she didn't have a partner or a spouse; no boyfriend, or girlfriend for that matter. She would end up being a wallflower and probably bored out of her mind... And yet! Perhaps she should go, if only for a short time – say an hour max. Just enough time to check everyone out. Maybe she could leave before she had to start explaining about her life and what she'd been up to since leaving school.

Melinda began thinking about herself. 'Her life! What about her life?'

Although she had been one of the seven Musketeers it had still been hard during the last of her school days. Melinda couldn't wait for school to finish so she could pack her bags and leave home. This she did, going to London to live with her Aunt Jenny – her mother's estranged sister.

By the time Melinda had reached her dizzy heights her aunts was waning. A few years later that lady had passed away. Her funeral had been one of the best ever attended in London with many titled gentlemen coming to pay their last respects to a woman they had all, at some time or another, known on a very personal level.

It was about that time that Melinda was fortunate enough to meet Simon.

Although he had been a few years older than her, being forty-nine to her twenty-seven they had got on very well together. Melinda knew she had become his trophy girlfriend but hadn't cared as she had truly loved him. Besides, he always took good care of her. Showering her with everything a girl from a poor family would ever want. Not that she needed anything, having made her own wealth by following in her Aunt's footsteps. Okay, so she did have to sleep with him! But, he was a gentleman when it came to being in bed. Making sure she enjoyed the experience as much as him. So, there were no regrets. He was also generous enough to let her continue running her expensive club (or she should say - brothel) as long as she reserved herself for only him. Which she readily agreed to do.

Finally, after many years together they had married in a quiet ceremony at a country house with only the necessary two witnesses. She had chosen that day to hand over control of her selective club to her protégé, Valerie. Melinda had been training her for some time, knowing the business would be in good hands. Her days as a Madame were done with. Or so she thought.

Simon and Melinda had been truly happy that first year. That was until he had suffered a heart attack one day. It had been a sad day but Melinda was happy she had had that last year with him. Fortunately, Simon had left her well provided for. There were no other relatives to inherit his fortune as his first wife and son had both died in a car accident sometime before they had met. She would live her life the way she wanted while overseeing her business from afar.

MELINDA

Goodbye Mom…

As far as Melinda was concerned her life was now
settled in London. Having once left the north she had
never returned. Not even to see her parents. Well, that
was, not until the day of her mother's funeral. She'd
felt guilty that day for not returning sooner. According
to her dad, her mother had been ill for a long time. He
told her she had been missed, but Melinda knew
differently. That was about all he had said to her.

Her older brother on the other hand had seemed
too pleased to see her, having had plenty to say. He
told her he was sorry she had not felt able to come
home before that day but said he understood why. The
way he looked at her, being as how she was now a
mature, well dressed, and certainly a beautiful sexy
woman proved to her that he had not forgotten the
horrors of his and Tom's attack on her. But then
neither had she. As he blatantly looked her up and
down, he went on to tell her she could have a bed at
his house, whilst they sorted things out and agreed the
arrangements of where she was finally going to live.

Melinda had to ask him twice what exactly he
meant by that comment. Eventually, and quite

petulantly, he had gone on at her about how she would have to move back up north, as she now had to look after their dad.

"After all," he kept repeating, "it's your duty to do so. And now you're all grown up, maybe we can have some more fun together?"

Melinda was gob-smacked at his audacity. He was married and here he was trying to seduce her.

Of course, he had been absolutely livid when she had turned on him, telling him in no uncertain terms what she thought of his offer. How sick she felt just looking at him. And, that there was no way she was returning to live in the North. It also took her some time to make him understand that she was in a committed relationship, and there was no way she was willing to give up her home or her lifestyle to look after the cantankerous, rude, bad-tempered man that was their Father. As far as she was concerned he could go into a home, especially if he was in so bad a state that he needed constant looking after. She went on to say that as regards having fun with him. Well, he could think again as was she never, ever going to be in close contact to such an evil bastard like him again. He made her sick.

Melinda had been quite adamant about it. Standing her ground, as there was no way she was returning north.

That night she had booked into a local hotel, spending the time walking around her old haunts. It had annoyed her that not once had they asked how she was, or what she had been doing with her life.

When she left the morning after the funeral, Melinda hadn't looked back. She knew she would never see her dad or her sick brother again. And, as expected, her older brother hadn't spoken another word to her since that day.

MELINDA

Moving on…

Having returned to London Melinda carried on with her life. She moved in with Simon and became the happiest she had ever been. The place of her birth had been wiped from Melinda's memory forever.

Or, so she had thought until opening the pink envelope. She looked at the invitation once again, remembering the smiling faces of the other Musketeers. There had been so much joy during the times spent with those girls. They had promised to stay in touch and yet hadn't she been eager to leave the town as soon as she could? Only Coleen had known what had happened.

'Why not go?' Melinda told herself. 'It might be amusing and interesting to see how everyone has turned out.'

She finished her sherry, giving the matter some more thought. Then, having finally decided to accept the invite she went and sat at her desk. Taking up her pen she began writing her reply…

Lady Melinda Priestly-Teddington (formerly Melinda Hammond) is pleased to acknowledge receipt of the invitation to attend the Class of '64 Reunion being held on 1st August.

Lady Priestly-Teddington will be both delighted and honoured to attend. She will not, however, be accompanied by A. N. Other.

Then scrawling her name across the bottom of the reply, she laughed out loud. "Let's see what Susie makes of that," and smiling she sealed the envelope before putting it in the basket for her assistant to post.

'It was certainly going to be an interesting reunion,' she thought, smiling to herself. It was the first time she had smiled since Simon had passed.

Thinking of him, she said, "You'll be with me, Simon, won't you? Holding my hand. I know you will."

PHILLIPA

Being dragged down…

Phillipa yawned; she was feeling rather tired this morning, much the same as she had every other morning. 'What am I doing here?' she thought. 'Same old same. Same old routine, day in, day out. Nothing ever seems to change.'

Her husband, Roland, had left the house early to miss the busy traffic on the motorway. He was going to be away on business, yet again; or at least he had said it was business.

"I'll be unobtainable this evening," he told her as he left the house. "I have a big meeting with some important clients. Out to dinner, then entertaining them afterward. Won't make it back tonight."

She had very nearly blurted out 'entertaining my eye' at him. But, as usual, she had kept her thoughts to herself, merely responding with a meek, "OK" and "Staying at the usual place I presume?" Before finishing with, "Have a nice time, dear."

Having given her an absent-minded peck on the cheek, before dashing outside and slamming the door behind him. Roland had left. Moments later, she had heard the sound of his car leaving the drive, before racing off down the street.

Not long afterward the kids had followed their father out of the house. Off to catch their bus to school.

'Kids!' thought Phillipa. 'How could a seventeen-year-old and a fifteen, nearly sixteen-year-old, be called kids.' She sighed. 'They seem to grow up so fast these days, and they think they know it all. Where have the years gone?'

Thinking about her life, she remembered how she and Roland had had such high hopes and big dreams when they were younger. They had planned on doing so many wonderful things. Going to different places, travelling the world, doing all the things they wanted to do before settling down. And, to some degree, they had achieved that, deciding they were going to enjoy life together for as long as they could. There would be no kids - just the two of them.

At the time they met, she was completing her after-school Secretarial studies. Once she had finished the course the pair had travelled to India where they had lived for six months, becoming wandering hippies.

After leaving India, they had spent the next eight months living and working in a Kibbutz in Israel. Life had been so good then. But where had all those dreams gone? When had the 'no kids policy' changed? Where were the memories of their travels, the places they saw, and the things they did together? She frowned as she tried to recall the exotic countries and sights they had seen and experienced.

All were distant memories now. Almost forgotten except in the photographs stashed away in the dusty albums hidden in the upstairs cupboard. Phillipa sighed sadly.

It had been whilst they were in Australia that they had received a distressing message from Roland's Mother. His father had suffered a mental breakdown. Roland was needed at home urgently to look after the business and his parents. And so, reluctantly, they had returned to Blighty and a normal lifestyle.

Moving into the Fitzpatrick family home, a very large five-bedroomed property on the edge of town, they had settled down to family life. Roland had begun running the family business, while Phillipa remained at home, looking after her in-laws. It was a terrible time for her. It was as if she had two grown-up children, and in a way, it had infuriated her. But, what could she do? This was her life now. She had wanted so desperately to recapture what she, no they, had lost, but deep inside she knew they never could. And so, life had gone on in a different vein.

PHILLIPA

A little ray of sunshine…

Suddenly the sound of the letterbox rattled as the postman pushed the mail through. There was a loud plop as it dropped to the hall floor, sounding as if there was a lot. Going into the hall to pick it up she thought it would probably be mostly junk mail. That's all they seemed to ever get these days. Besides, who would want to write to her?

She was lucky if her step-sister sent her a short note once a year. And when she did, it was usually only at Christmas time when she would write: 'Just a quick line to catch up.'

That was how she had always started the note attached to the posh Xmas card. It was always a 'short note,' usually telling Phillipa how well she was doing, or what they had been up to. Or that Mervin, her husband, had bought her a new fur coat, a new car, or that they were going to visit China, America, or Australia. There was never a, 'how are you, Sis,' or 'I miss you, Sis' or 'let's get together sometime soon, Sis.'

'Some sister you are,' thought Phillipa as she sorted the post. She noted there was the usual assortment of envelopes - gas bill, credit card bill, charity begging letter, etc. But there, in the middle of the pile, was a pink envelope? And it was addressed to Miss Phillipa Thomson!

Surprised, she looked at the envelope again. Phillipa Thomson! No one had called her that in over 20 years. Maybe her sister had re-directed it on to her?

Carefully slitting the envelope open she slowly pulled out the card. Turning it over she saw it was an invitation to a forthcoming reunion on the 1st of August. Partners were welcome but could she RSVP as soon as possible.

Taking the invitation into the kitchen she placed it on the table, made herself a cup of coffee then sat down to stare at the card.

'A reunion at my old school,' she thought.

She sat and thought about the invitation long and hard. She would love to go but knew she probably wouldn't. For a start, Roland would flatly refuse to do consider anything she suggested or agree to do anything she wanted to do. Besides, she had nothing suitable to wear! Which she knew was a stupid, silly excuse because she could always buy something new.

No! If she was truthful, she was actually too frightened to go. She felt such a frump these days. She would feel out of place. Besides, people would probably pity her and she couldn't stand that. No! She was determined she wasn't going to go.

"Might as well throw the card straight in the bin and forget all about it," she said out loud, and taking the invitation she went towards the kitchen waste bin. Yet, for some reason she couldn't quite explain, she dropped the card into the cutlery drawer instead. As she did so the phone began ringing, so slamming the drawer shut she raced to answer it.

A short while later Phillipa replaced the receiver, swearing as she did.

"Damn, damn, damn."

That had been Roland, telling her he wouldn't be home tomorrow after all. He had to stay on for another day so he wouldn't be back now until late Sunday evening! With the kids leaving on their school trip early in the morning it meant Phillipa would be on her own over the weekend.

"Don't complain," she told herself sighing. "At least now you can have some 'me' time. You can do the things you want to do for a change, instead of being at the beck and call of others."

PHILLIPA

Life is irritating…

Early the following morning, Phillipa waved the boys off. They were excited about being away from home for a week.

Over the next couple of days, no matter how much she tried to chivvy herself up with the idea of being able to do her own thing, Phillipa, for some unexplainable reason, felt lost and lonely. She felt dejected, and despite her unexpected freedom, she went around the house all weekend in a depressed state.

Roland rang again Saturday evening to tell her he wouldn't be home on Sunday after all, so not to expect him back until late Monday, although it could probably be Tuesday night' but even then he wasn't really sure exactly which day it would be. Phillipa didn't respond.

Returning from shopping on Monday afternoon, Phillipa thought about how the house always appeared empty these days. The thought left her feeling low.

"Pull yourself together girl," she told her reflection in the kitchen window as she washed the pots. "Have a coffee and relax."

Going to the drawer for a spoon she spotted the invitation, still lying where she had dropped it. Picking it up she thought about the girls she had known at school; the Musketeers. There had been Melinda, Fran, Coleen, Susie, Lorraine, Zhora and herself. All seven had been members of the school netball team. But, more importantly, they had been her special friends!

"So special," Phillipa snorted out loudly, "that we all lost touch shortly after leaving school."

Phillipa remembered how Melinda couldn't wait to leave school, and how she had quickly gone off to London to find and marry a rich husband. Susie had caused quite a stir by marrying Teddy Smith. He had been a bit of a tear-away at school but must have changed after marrying Susie, as Phillipa had never heard anything bad about him again. As it happened, Susie turned out to be pregnant when they married. Fran had joined the Army - a lifelong ambition of hers. Whilst poor Zhora had known she would have an arranged marriage waiting for her.

But, it was Lorraine who had surprised them all by joining the Police force, even managing to rise up the ranks to that of Inspector, according to the newspapers.

Phillipa laughed out loudly as she remembered Lorraine. "What an air-head she had been. Often bringing the whole class to stitches with her comments. She had been the typical dizzy blonde back then."

As for Coleen, she had gone back to Ireland. She had been sent to live with her Aunt in England because of the troubles back home. Following the death of her mother, her dad had wanted Colleen kept safe, but as soon as she was eighteen nothing, and no one, was going to keep Coleen locked up in a strange country away from her family. And so, she had gone back to Ireland at the first opportunity without a backward glance.

'And what did you do?' thought Phillipa.

Well, she'd fallen for the first good-looking bloke who had come along and swept her off her feet. Roland Fitzpatrick. And boy, her Roland had turned out to be a real smoothie. And, if truth be told he still was to this day. He'd changed slightly as he'd got older. Or maybe, it was her who'd changed?

The days were gone when she could no longer ignore the fact that he was always looking at younger women. He thought he was doing it slyly but she always saw him doing it. But, she had never pulled him up about it.

'Perhaps I should have said something; too late now,' she thought.

PHILLIPA

Choices and decisions…

Looking at the card, Phillipa re-read the details of the invitation. Maybe she should go? Why not? Besides, it would be great to meet up with the girls again. After all, they had always been together whilst at school, even when not playing netball.

Phillipa mulled it over for a while, then finally she came to a decision. She would go to the reunion. However, she realised she needed to ring Roland to ensure he would be free on that date, as she wanted him to go with her. She knew he would grumble about it but she had decided to insist on them both attending. Besides, she rarely asked him to do anything for her, so this time he could make the effort.

With her mind settled, Phillipa went to the phone and picking up the receiver she rang the hotel, asking for Mr. Roland Fitzpatrick's room. There was a short pause before it began ringing.

'Perhaps he's out,' she thought. But, after about five rings the phone was answered. Only it wasn't the voice she'd been expecting to hear.

"Hello," said the person on the other end of the line.

For a moment Phillipa froze. Shocked by the response. It was a woman's voice; soft, deep and husky.

"Hello," the voice repeated. "Is anyone there?"

Stammering, Phillipa said the first thing that came into her mind. "Is, is, that Coleen Edwards, please?"

"No," replied the sexy voice, "this is Mrs. Fitzpatrick, you must have the wrong extension."

Phillipa started shaking and without waiting, she muttered a meek apology and hung up.

Her head was spinning. So much so, that she had to sit down on the stairs to gather her thoughts, which were suddenly all over the place. Slowly she replayed the call over in her head, not understanding what had happened. The voice had said she was... Mrs. Fitzpatrick.

'No, that's wrong. I'm Mrs. Fitzpatrick,' thought Phillipa. Then she said the words out loud, "She can't be Mrs. Fitzpatrick. Because... I'm Mrs. Fitzpatrick."

Slowly she started searching her mind. Trying to remember if Roland had any relatives living in the area near to the hotel! But, deep down she knew there were none. Suddenly the phone started ringing, making her jump in shock. Phillipa stared at the instrument as if it was evil. Almost as if it was going to attack her. The ringing seemed to be getting shriller and shriller. Pick me up it was insisting – pick me up, pick me up!

Taking a deep breath, Phillipa reached out with a shaking hand towards the receiver just as the noise stopped. The silence was as deafening as the ringing had been. Turning away from the phone she caught sight of her reflection in the hall mirror. It was as if a stranger was staring back at her. A white-faced, shaking stranger.

"You should have guessed," she whispered to her reflection. "Why didn't you realise what was happening?" All those nights away on business. The distant feeling that had slowly sprung up between them. "My God," she whispered, "what am I going to do. I need a drink," and she headed back towards the kitchen.

Sitting at the kitchen table, she played the whole scenario over again in her mind, before finally admitting that she had seen the signs but had chosen to ignore them. The lack of communication. The fact they hardly went out anywhere together and, of course, worse still, no familiarity, no sex. Roland must have got bored and looked to spice up his life.

Mulling it over, Phillipa finally asked herself, "Can I blame him? Not really. After all, it is as much my fault as his." Then it suddenly dawned on her, perhaps the time had come for her to make some major decisions and choices with her life. The question was, what?

She had just started to calm down when the phone started ringing again. Going into the hall she carefully picked up the receiver, her heart pounding loudly in her breast. Then she heard her husband's voice come on the line.

"H.. Hi... D... Darling," he sounded hesitant, as well as a little apprehensive. "Did... you... try ringing me?"

Phillipa knew this was decision time. Taking only a matter of seconds to gather her thoughts together, she spoke. In a surprisingly calm voice, she told him, "No dear, but whilst you are on the line please make a note in your diary for the 1st August. I have been invited to a reunion at my old school and I've decided that I, we," (and she put an emphasis on the word 'we') "are going, so please make sure you don't book anything else for that weekend."

There was a short pause before, Roland sighing with relief, readily agreed to her request.

In response, Phillipa said, "That's good, thank you. Oh, and by the way, please don't be late home tomorrow, will you? I plan on us going out for tea, seeing as how the boys are away until Wednesday. I presume that is okay with you?"

Her husband, sensing a firmness in his wife's voice he had not heard for some time, agreed without further comment, after which Phillipa replaced the phone.

Returning to the kitchen, she took up the invitation once again. Then finding a notelet she wrote her acceptance.

'Yes,' she thought smiling to herself. 'There are choices and decisions to be made and I am certainly going to start making them, in due course - but for now, I will wait. Whilst the kids are still here, I will just wait. But, the day will come when they will be ready to leave home. And when they do, so will I, Roland. So, in the meantime, I will prepare myself.'

COLEEN

Time to stand up…

"You can't go girl. You're not capable of managing on your own," ranted her brother.

"That I am," Coleen stormed back at him. "I'm more than capable." And she stared back at her brother as he stood glaring at her. He was fuming. "Why can't you leave me alone" she cried out.

"There's no talking to you, girl," her brother came back, then turning towards his father he said, "Talk some sense into her, da'? She won't listen to me!"

Throughout the outburst, their Father had remained silent. Slowly he looked up from his newspaper and calmly thought before responding to his son's comment.

"She's a big girl and her own mistress. She'll do what she wants, regardless of you or me, so leave her be and stop all the shouting." Then he calmly returned to reading his newspaper as if, having spoken, that was the end of the matter.

Her brother looked at her stony-faced, then turning sharply he quickly frog-marched out of the house. Coleen looked towards her Father, then gently said, "Thanks, Da', for not having a go at me."

Her father lowered his paper again and looked at her for a moment. He smiled, gently shaking his head before returning to his newspaper without uttering another word. Taking his unspoken message to heart Coleen turned and headed for her room, leaving him to read in peace.

Once in her room, she picked up the invitation and re-read it – Class of 64 Reunion.

'Why can't I go?' she thought. There was no reason why not. She would take a few days and make it a holiday, as the event was being held in the small town where she had spent most of her senior school years, quite a distance from her home in Ireland.

Coleen had gone to England following the death of her mother. It had been a sad time for her family as her Mother's passing had been due to a heart attack, brought on by the loss of her aunt, her mother's sister. Coleen's Aunt had been travelling north to visit her daughter who lived in Belfast when she had been caught up in a shooting incident at a border crossing.

The loss of his sister-in-law, and then his wife shortly afterwards, had aged her father. She knew he would never forgive that element of the IRA for their involvement in their deaths.

The local IRA representative had visited the house to offer sympathies but her father had sent the man packing, cursing him and all those involved in the whole affair. Not long after her father had decided it would be safer for Coleen to leave Ireland. And so he had arranged for his daughter to travel to the North of England to live with his sister. Despite begging to stay, Coleen had had no option but to leave.

Arriving at Old Brampton School, Coleen had been surprised at how quickly she had been welcomed into the small group of girls known as the 'Musketeers.' And once they discovered she could play netball, she was actively encouraged to become a team member. While she missed her family deeply, she could not complain about being lonely.

'They weren't bad years,' she thought. 'I made some good friends, and I did enjoy the time living at my Aunts house.'

But she had missed her home, the beautiful land of her birth. So, when the school had finished Coleen couldn't wait to return to Ireland. It had been wonderful to see her da' and her brother again. Even though he railed at her, she still loved her brother dearly. Life had been good back then and she had soon put her days in England far behind her.

COLEEN

Memories that hurt...

Whilst the invitation had brought back some lovely memories these were quickly followed by some deeply sad ones. It had been a few months after returning home that Coleen had met Daniel. She couldn't help but smile as she remembered their first meeting. He'd had the most gorgeous deep blue eyes she had ever seen in a man; and a smile that had made her heart flutter madly. Also, the lilt in his voice had been softly captivating. They had started dating shortly afterwards. Life had seemed so perfect back then.

That was until the day Danny told her he was going away.

"Where?" she cried. "Why?"

Carefully Danny had explained he was going north to Derry to look for work.

"But it's not safe there," she told him. "I'll come with you."

He had been very gentle, telling Coleen in strong terms, that no she couldn't.

"Besides," he told her, he needed time to get settled, find some work, and a place for them to live.

She had cried but he had held her in his arms,

doing his best to reassure her that they would be together very soon. Finally, having convinced her it would be better if he went alone, he told her it would give him the chance to raise enough money so they could get married. Reluctantly Coleen had agreed with everything he had told her.

A few days later Daniel was gone, having promised to write to her twice a week. And he had. Or at least for the first month or two. He'd even rung her at the local pub every Saturday night, as they had no phone at home. The calls were always the same. Telling her how much he loved her, how much he missed her, and that as soon as he got work, he would send for her.

Coleen had cried each time he rang, and when she asked him how soon they would be together, he would only say, "Soon, very soon."

By the end of the second month, the letters started to arrive every other week. Then the phone calls had stopped being as regular.

When they did talk, he still kept on reassuring her, saying how much he loved her, and she, the foolish girl that she was, had continued in believing him. But there were moments when they were talking on the phone, that she thought she could hear a girl's voice in the background. He had brushed her questions aside, telling her not to be so foolish or jealous. Saying it was just the TV in the next room. And because

Coleen loved him, she had innocently accepted his reassurances without further question.

By the fourth month, the letters and phone calls had stopped altogether. Coleen wrote a number of letters asking Danny what was wrong. Why hadn't he been in touch with her? But there was no reply to any of them. Finally, she couldn't stand it anymore, deciding to travel north to find him. Telling her da' what she planned to do and where she was going, Coleen left for Derry a few days later.

To Coleen, Londonderry seemed such a cold place, nothing at all like her small hometown. She couldn't understand why Danny would want to stay here. It took her quite some time to find the address where he lived. Walking down the street she eventually found number eleven. Standing looking at the place, she thought it looked like a squat.

Finally, knocking on the door, she waited expectantly. But when it opened, she was shocked to see, not her Danny but a tall girl with long blonde hair. The girl looked at her before asking what she wanted. Coleen explained she was looking for Danny. The girl told her he wasn't in but he was due back so she could come in and wait for him. Curious as to who this person was, Coleen followed the young woman into the house. She was unaware of the smirk that crossed the other girl's face. Feeling a little uncomfortable

Coleen sat down in a chair to await Danny's return. She didn't have long to wait when shortly afterwards the sound of the front door banging made her jump. Then she heard Danny's voice calling out, "It's only me, me darling."

Coleen froze, surprised at his familiarity. As he walked into the room, the blonde girl had a big grin across her face. Seeing Coleen sitting in the chair, Danny stopped dead in his tracks.

After a short pause, he suddenly began shouting.

"What the hell are you doing here? Why have you come? Why didn't you tell me you were coming?"

Coleen was shocked and terrified by his reaction. Before Danny could say anything more, she jumped up and ran for the door. A very distressed Coleen was last seen running down the street with Danny chasing after her, calling out her name.

How long or how far she ran, Coleen could not remember, but when she finally stopped and calmed down, she knew she had nowhere to go other than back home. It was just as she turned towards the railway station that there was a white flash and a loud bang.

Suddenly, she felt as if she was flying through the air, before she began falling, falling until finally nothing but blackness. That was the last thing she remembered.

Coleen was unconscious for over a week. When

she finally opened her eyes, it took her a while to gather her senses. Slowly turning her head, she discovered her father and brother sitting, smiling at her.

"Welcome back, Mavourneen," said her father gently. "We thought you were going to leave us," and he leaned over to kiss her tenderly on the forehead.

The warmth of the all too familiar voice and his tenderness caused Coleen to break down. Later, once she was strong enough, she managed to tell them what she remembered had happened. Or at least as much as she could recall.

Her brother had wanted to throttle Danny, deciding he would go to try and find him. When he returned later that day he was accompanied by the Garda. They asked Coleen a lot of questions and she told them everything she could remember.

Much later, she was shocked and surprised to discover that the house where Danny had been living was an IRA safe house. A place where bombs were manufactured. Bombs similar to the one which had exploded close to her. It turned out that Danny, her blue-eyed gentle man, had become a terrorist. Her heart had been broken that day. But not just her heart.

Some weeks later Coleen returned home accompanied by her father and brother - only now she was in a wheelchair. Her legs had been damaged in the blast and Coleen knew she would never walk again. It had been a very hard time, especially for her father, but somehow, they had all managed to learn to cope.

Danny, of course, was never heard of again. What had happened to him no-one knew. There had been some bodies from the blast which couldn't be identified. Coleen knew she would never forgive him for what he had done to her. It was hoped by all that eventually time would heal the wounds of her heart, as the wounds of her body had healed.

* * * * *

The ringing of the clock sounding in the hall caused Coleen to return to the present. The invitation was still in her hand. There was no reason why she couldn't go? She was old enough and more than capable. However, she would ask her cousin Mary to go with her. Hopefully, they could stay at her Aunts place for a few days. It would be nice to catch up as she hadn't seen her in a long time.

With her mind finally made up, Coleen returned to the lounge and told her father, "I've had a rethink about the invitation, Da'." He looked up but didn't speak. She continued, "I've decided I'm going to go to England but… I'll take our Mary with me, so you don't need to worry. That way, you'll know I'm in safe hands," and she smiled at him.

Her father looked at her, and smiling he nodded his head in agreement.

"Okay. Good idea, Mavourneen," all the while thinking, 'That's my girl, that's my brave girl.'

FRANCIS
(Known as FRAN)

End of an era...

"ATTENTION! Officer present!" shouted the Corporal.

The room quickly stood to attention as Fran entered. Walking slowly past the members of her platoon, she inspected each one of them carefully. For some reason she found herself becoming overwhelmed with emotion. These were her troops. The men and women she had trained with, patrolled with, eaten with, and even fought alongside. They were an excellent bunch. Yet here she was, making her last inspection. It was a sad time for her; but still, the pride in them shone through.

Having walked the length of the room and back again without saying a word, she finally took a deep breath.

"At ease. Firstly, I want to thank you all for your loyalty, your friendship, and your comradeship over these last few years. We've been through some tough times, even some frightening ones, but we've also had some happy times together. I just wanted to say... how honoured and proud I am to have served with each, and every one of you."

Pausing, she took a deep breath, in order to stem her rising emotions, then continued, "As you are aware my time is up, and I am returning to civvies. But, just because I'm leaving doesn't mean you can start to slack off or let your standards drop. I trust you will give your new CO the same level of comradeship and support that you have given me. So, once again I thank you and please, take care of yourselves. All of you!"

As she finished speaking the Corporal stepped forward and spoke. "Captain, on behalf of the troops I would like to say it's been an honour and a privilege to have served with you. You have shown us what a CO should be like. Treated us all fairly and respectfully. Three cheers for the Captain. Hip hip… - *Hooray* – Hip hip… *Hooray* – Hip hip… *Hooray*."

"Thank you." Fran smiled at them all. They were a grand bunch and she was sad to be leaving.

On that note, the Corporal shouted, "**Attention**."

Whereupon Fran smartly saluted her platoon, before turning on her heels and marching out of the barracks for the last time.

Back in her quarters, Fran slowly finished packing her personal effects. This was a sad time for her. After all, the Army had been her life for the past twenty years. But, they didn't want her anymore. What she was going to do she didn't know?

As she looked around her quarters, she thought, 'That's the only problem with the Army. They want you when you're young, so they can mould you to suit them. They use you but, when your time is up, they drop you without a backward glance.'

Not that that was really true, after all, she had been offered a promotion and a desk job. But it wasn't really for her, and regardless of her sadness at leaving, she knew the years spent in the forces had in reality been extremely happy ones for her. However, now it was time for her to go.

Being in the army, Fran had been fortunate enough to travel the world. Sometimes the postings were good ones, occasionally they could be dangerous. Not that she had minded. Wherever the posting, she had taken it all in her stride. But the last place had been the worst.

It had been during her recent sojourn abroad that Fran and her unit had been caught in the crossfire. Despite having three wounded men her troops had done exceptionally well. They had also managed to carry their wounded out safely, escaping with only minor injuries.

She too had been wounded, ending up in hospital for a couple of months. Fortunately, it hadn't been too serious and she was now fully recovered. That was one side of army life she certainly wouldn't miss.

Gathering up her civvies she began to change, folding her uniform and laying it on the bed. That was something Fran wouldn't be keeping. Well, only her dress uniform as she was due to attend an award ceremony. The team had been mentioned in despatches and all were to be given medals for their gallantry. Her adjutant would return everything else to the stores on her behalf.

As she picked up her blouse, Fran noticed the pink envelope lying on the edge of the bed. She had forgotten all about her mail. 'A pink envelope! I bet that had the boys in the post room talking,' thought Fran, laughing to herself. She could just imagine what they would have said. Such as, 'Hey, lads look at this. The stony Captain's got a pink envelope. Hmmm, even smells nice. Perhaps she's a lesbian after all, eh?'

Laughing again, she thought, 'It takes all sorts!'

Yet really, she couldn't blame them for thinking any different. She had always been a soldier first, through and through. There were no frills on her. She was a tough, no-nonsense 'bitch' that wouldn't let anyone take advantage of her. She'd been like that because that was the only way for a woman to achieve success in this man's army. And success is what she had aspired to. But that was all behind her now. She faced a new start. There was a new life was waiting for her outside the barrack doors. The question though was what would it be?

Throwing the envelope into her case, she closed and locked it. Taking one more look around the room that had been home for such a long time, she opened the door and swiftly left. Climbing into her car she drove towards the barracks gate. As she passed through, the soldier on duty saluted her for the last time. Then turning left onto the main road she headed north, not taking time to look back.

FRANCIS
(Known as FRAN)

Welcome home…

Three hours later, Fran pulled into the driveway of her parent's home. Stepping out of the car she looked at the familiar house that had always been her base when home on leave. It felt both good, and sad, to be back. Suddenly the front door was flung open and her father stepped out, laughingly asking her, "Are you coming in, or are you still thinking about it, Franny?"

Leaving the car, she smiled at his use of the old familiar name, before going forward to hug him, and replying, "Well, actually, I was thinking what colour we could repaint the house. What do you think? Red, blue, or maybe yellow?" And they both began laughing at her comment.

After standing together for a few seconds looking at the house, Fran wickedly asked, "What about khaki, Dad. Do you think Mom would agree to that? I know where I can get some paint, real cheap!"

Her father didn't reply but he continued laughing until a voice sounded from the doorway. "Are you two going to stand on the doorstep all day, or are you coming in. I have tea and sandwiches ready for you," announced her Mother, waiting to receive a hug from her only daughter.

With the greetings over the three of them made their way into the dining room, where they sat down to enjoy the refreshments her Mother had prepared. An hour later, Fran took her cases upstairs and settled into her old room. Her parents had never changed the colour scheme. Keeping it looking girlie, with all her childhood mementoes scattered around.

Later that night as Fran lay in bed, she thought how strange it felt to be back once more in her old bed. It wasn't until the early hours that she finally fell into a deep sleep.

Sleeping in wasn't an option for Fran. After all her body clock was set to Army time so, the following morning, she was up bright and early. Not wanting to wake her parents she spent the time going through her cases, sorting and hanging her clothes and other stuff. At a sensible time, she made her way downstairs.

During breakfast, her Father asked, "So, what do you intend doing, now you've left the forces?"

Fran thought for a moment before answering. "To be honest, Dad, at the moment I'm not sure what I want to do. I do have one or two things in mind, but I need to do some research first before I decide."

In reality, Fran didn't want to worry her parents about her not having any definitive plans. Having received a good pay-out from her job she had quite a large balance in her savings account so knew that money wouldn't be a problem for the immediate future. "For the moment I am going to take a holiday while I look at my options," she told them. "I do have enough money to pay for my upkeep."

"We don't want your money, sweetie," replied her mother. "All we are concerned about is that you are happy. You know you are welcome to stay here. This is your home, so take as long as you like."

If truth be known, Fran was quite happy to take her parents up on their offer. But she also knew she wouldn't want to put on them for too long. Besides, she was too independent and needed to live her life her way.

FRANCIS
(Known as FRAN)

Old haunts…

Over the next few days, Fran spent her time visiting old haunts; which meant it was some time before she remembered the pink envelope. Taking the card out, she re-read the invitation to the Reunion; realising it was to take place in a few days.

'The question is,' she asked herself, 'do I want to attend or not?'

She hadn't planned on going, but perhaps she should? Although it would feel strange to be attending a civvies event. At least if she went to the party, she could catch up with her old school friends whom she hadn't seen since leaving Old Brampton Senior School.

While she'd been walking around her local area, Fran had noted the old school building had gone; seemingly having been pulled down some years previously. The grounds and playing fields had been converted into a new housing estate. It now contained a large number of modern townhouses and semi-detached properties. To Fran, they looked too clinical and box-like.

As she had stood staring at the old grounds, the memories of her school days had come flooding back. She began remembering the six special girls whom she had been close to at school. The seven of them had all been members of the school netball team. They'd been pretty close throughout school time, even being nicknamed the 'Musketeers' by the teachers. The girls had told each other everything, their most intimate secrets, including what they wanted to be when they grew up. In reality, they had all had their own ideas about what they thought they would do once they left school. But Fran had kept quiet about her plans, not wanting her friends to make fun of her. Not that they would have done so. Mind you, they were certainly surprised when she had finally told them she was joining the army. But that was a long time ago.

Fran recalled the day she had gone to sign up. Her father had accompanied her to the enrolment office. Although both parents were reluctant, they had acceded to her wishes, her father signing the consent forms without question. He would often blame his mother for talking about his father and him being a war hero as he believed that was her Fran had got the idea of the army from. And it was true she had got the idea from learning about her Grandfather.

It was many years later before her father finally accepted that the army had always been Fran's one desire, her calling; even after she was wounded. Mind you, her parents heaved a big sigh of relief, when she informed them she was finally leaving the army. It was a decision she did not regret, believing that her army days had been as good as her school days. After all, in both areas, she'd formed good friends, and received comradeship. Much the same as when she had played in the school netball team.

FRANCIS
(Known as FRAN)

The decision is made...

Later that day back in her room, Fran went to the cupboard and took out the school yearbook. Turning to the pages containing the images of her school friends, she thought how young and innocent they had all looked.

Recalling that last day at school Fran remembered giving each of the seven Musketeers a small gift. Susie got a small pendant with a dolphin on, her favourite animal. Fran gave Melinda a notebook and pen as she was always making notes, usually about netball tactics. To Phillipa, she had given her a button brooch made from a woven fabric of mixed pink colours. Pink was Phillipa's favourite colour at the time. Coleen had received a small silver crucifix, and to Lorraine, she had given her a lovely black, fountain pen.

Zhora had been the hardest one to buy for; her being Asian. Besides, Fran hadn't been sure if her family would approve of her receiving gifts. However, after a lot of thought, she had finally settled on giving her friend a lovely headscarf, which Zhora had loved.

Or so she said. Fran suddenly wondered if they would remember her. Surprisingly, she hoped so.

Replacing the book in the cupboard, Fran went downstairs to tell her parents about the reunion, surprising her mother by asking her to go shopping with her. She wanted to buy a nice dress and some new shoes for the event. Having mainly worn khaki for the last twenty years she knew fashions had changed, so decided she would need some help in choosing clothes that would suit her. The idea of spending time shopping with her daughter certainly delighted her mother. As such, plans were quickly made for the following day.

* * * * *

Returning home, the following afternoon, Fran felt a little giddy. Despite herself, she had enjoyed shopping with her mother. This was something they hadn't done together in a long time.

Her choice of dress and shoes had left her feeling happy that she had decided to go to the reunion. She was now determined to make every effort to enjoy the event. Besides, it was going to be something different from what she was used to. Her one hope was that she would find her long-lost friends welcoming her warmly. She was sure they would.

160

ZHORA

Petulance is stressful…

"Salaam, Ammi," Zhora called out as she entered the house, closing the door firmly behind her.

There was no reply. She sighed. It appeared her Mother was going to be difficult again. "It's me, Ammi," she tried again as she removed her coat. Still no response.

Hanging her coat on a peg near the hall mirror, Zhora quickly checked her hair before turning and lifting the mail from the metal basket that hung behind the front door. Quickly she checked the names on the envelopes, ensuring that any addressed to her late father were put with those for her brother Saleem. Even after all this time, the post needed to be checked before her Mother read it as sometimes there were odd letters addressed to her deceased parent which would distress her.

Flicking through the pile of envelopes Zhora stopped, surprised at the sight of a pink envelope, but more startled to see her name written on it. Why would someone write to her?

Hearing her mother moving about in the back sitting room, Zhora quickly slipped the envelope into her coat pocket before continuing down the hallway and going into the room.

"You took your time," announced her Mother petulantly.

"Yes, sorry, I was sorting the mail," answered Zhora as she handed her mother an envelope addressed to her, before placing the rest of the mail on the shelf above the fireplace. She knew her younger brother would check them when he returned home later in the day.

"Have you eaten yet?" asked Zhora. "Would you like a cup of tea?"

Her mother sniffed loudly before responding sharply. "Of course, I've eaten. I may be old but I am not incapable of doing things for myself. Besides, Parveen made sure I had something. She's a good girl that Parveen."

'Meaning I'm not,' thought Zhora, sighing quietly.

Zhora liked her sister-in-law but often felt sorry that she had to live in the same house as her mother-in-law. However, she was also getting fed up with always being told what 'a good girl Parveen was.'

"Well, I'm having a cup of tea, do you want one or not?" she asked, doing her best to keep the annoyance under control and out of her voice.

"Yes," replied her Mother sharply, all the while carrying on watching the movie, she had put in the DVD player.

Going into the kitchen, Zhora made a pot of tea for the two of them, before returning to the room where she placed a cup on the table next to where her mother sat. There was no acknowledgment or thank you.

Sitting down on the sofa she drank her tea. The silence of the room only being broken by the noise of the television. Once she had finished, Zhora stood up, and taking the empty cups into the kitchen she washed them out, leaving them to drain on the side.

Having done her duty, Zhora was now ready to leave the house. Turning to her Mother she asked, "Do you want me to take you shopping this week?" There was no response. "Ammi, did you hear me?" she asked a little louder.

"I heard you," snarled her mother, "Are you sure you can spare the time?"

Zhora sighed, once more doing her best to control her temper. Why did they have to go through this same routine every week? It was almost as if she was begging her mother to take notice of her.

"Well," she asked patiently. "Do you want to go shopping or not? If you do then I need to know which day and what time as I have a lot on this week. I also have lots of meetings with clients."

"So, it's too much trouble to take your mother shopping," replied her parent sarcastically, "After all, your work is more important than your poorly, sick mother."

This time Zhora couldn't hold her tongue, replying sharply, "That is not true. And you are not sick or poorly. I have just asked you if you want to go shopping, but all you do is moan."

"Oh, that's it. Have a go at your poor mother. Rashid wouldn't have treated me this way. He would have done anything for his mother," her parent replied snidely.

That was the last straw for Zhora, as she angrily replied, "Oh yes, your precious Rashid would have done things for you, wouldn't he? I think not. Have you not noticed, Mother, that your dear Rashid isn't here to do anything for you? Or anyone else for that matter."

"Don't you dare speak of your brother in that way," snapped her mother. "He was a good son?"

At her mother's outburst, Zhora finally let her temper overtake her sense of control. "A good son! A good son! Where the hell have you been living these last few years? Your so-called good son caused the death of thirty-seven people. On top of that, he ruined his wife and his children's lives **and**, he caused my father to die from a broken heart. Oh no, **mother**, your wonderful Rashid was most certainly **not**… a good… son… at all…"

Suddenly the air was filled with a loud scream, as in anger, her mother yelled, "How dare you. At least he married properly. You walked away from your upbringing and your religion. You married that, that man. Get out. I don't need your help."

By this time, Zhora had had enough. She knew she had to leave before things got out of hand. She was sick and tired of her mother having a go at her about her husband, so all she said was, "Don't worry I'm going. You are so bigoted that you've never even given Ray a chance."

Then taking a deep, calming breath, she continued, "At least he loves me and looks after me. Which is a hell of a lot more than your precious, Rashid ever did for you, my father, or his wife and kids! And as for your lovely son, Saleem. Well, he treats his wife like a bloody slave. Perhaps if you opened your bloody eyes for once and stopped being so damned selfish you might see how unhappy Parveen really is. Maybe then you would see what rotten sons you gave birth to."

Her daughter's outburst had shocked her Mother; for once leaving her speechless. Zhora had never dared speak to her like that before. How dare she? About to turn and say something she found she was too late as Zhora had left the room.

ZHORA

A calming influence…

Collecting her bag and coat Zhora stormed out of the house, slamming the front door behind her as loudly as she could. Sitting in her car, she realised she was shaking. It was true she had never spoken to her Mother like that before. And yet, there had been so many times when she had wanted to tell her the truth about her favourite son, Rashid.

Suddenly her phone rang. Picking it up she saw it was her husband.

"Hello, sweetheart," she said breathlessly.

"Are you okay, darling?" asked Ray questioningly. "Where are you? Have you been running?"

Taking a deep breath, she replied, "No. I'm sat in the car outside Moms. I'm afraid I lost my temper with her and stormed out before I said too much."

"Did you argue over me?" asked her husband laughingly.

Laughing back, Zhora responded, "No, my darling. This time it was about Rashid. I'm afraid I was a bit too blunt."

"Oh, dear! Do you want to talk about it?"

"Not now, maybe later."

"Okay sweetie, what about meeting me for lunch? Shall we say twelve-thirty at the cafe?"

Agreeing to the 'date' with her husband, Zhora hung up.

Having calmed down and stopped shaking she fastened her seat belt and started the car. She took one last look towards her parent's home, to see if her mother was watching her. But it was difficult to tell if she was standing behind the curtains or not. Finally checking her mirror, she slowly moved out into the traffic.

Just before twelve-thirty, Zhora pulled her car into a parking space near their favourite cafe. Entering the building, she looked for her husband, noticing him sitting in the corner studying the menu. As she approached, he looked up, almost as if he had sensed her presence. As she reached the table he stood, took her coat, and held out a chair ready for her to sit down.

'What a difference there was between Asian men and English ones,' she thought. Well, at least there was a difference with this English man. He was such a gentleman. Pulling out the seat, holding the door open for her, standing whenever she came into the room. Yes, he was a real gentleman; something she was still not used to, despite the years they'd been married.

"Bad morning, sweetheart?" asked her husband

gently as he kissed her on the cheek in greeting.

She smiled warmly. "Yes, but I don't want to talk about her. So, what are we going to order?"

Taking the cue from his wife, Ray quickly changed the subject. He knew she would tell him everything about the morning but only in her own good time. So for now, he was quite content to just enjoy her company and make small chit-chat about other things.

An hour later they left the café, each going their separate ways. Ray returned to his office where he worked as a solicitor and Zhora to her own business where she designed up-market clothing for well-to-do Asian and Oriental women. Both of them being highly successful in their chosen careers.

ZHORA

Good memories…

It wasn't until she arrived at her office that Zhora finally discovered the pink envelope sitting in her coat pocket. Taking it out she opened it, surprised by the invitation. She hadn't thought about her school for years. Although, as she read the details on the card, the memories came flooding back.

She began recalling the group of girls with whom she had been close friends during those carefree years. It had been unusual for Asian girls to mix with the English ones at that time but those girls had been wonderful, easily welcoming her into their merry band. She had been surprised that they had allowed her to join them but they had.

Her father had allowed her to join the netball team, much against her mother's wishes. He had seen how good she was at the game, and being an all-girls team, he was more than happy to allow her to play. The only condition was that she wore trousers. The school had agreed, and so Zhora had worn the school's sports colours over the top of her clothes. So close had the girls become that their group had been nicknamed the 'Musketeers' by the teachers. The name had stuck, causing Zhora to take time to find out more about the infamous historical fighters, enjoying what she had learnt about them.

In truth, Zhora had been sad that last day at school. She felt that her life would never be as happy or as carefree as it had been during those school years. Although her father had been quite liberal her mother was the opposite, never allowing her to invite any of the girls to their home.

She remembered that Fran had been exceptionally nice, even giving her a beautiful headscarf as a memento of their friendship. Zhora had sneaked the scarf into the house, hiding it at the bottom of her drawer. Occasionally she would take it out, wearing it in the privacy of her room. When she married, she took it with her, wearing it all she could.

During those last few days, the other girls had all talked about what they wanted to do when they left school. Zhora had always wanted to be a fashion designer but believed she would never achieve such an ambition. Well, back then she hadn't. No, for her it was to be an arranged marriage. That's what her mother had planned for her. Strangely her father hadn't agreed, doing all he could to divert her mother from such action. He actively encouraged his daughter in attending college where she could learn more about sewing, etc. As it turned out by the time her mother found someone whom Zhora could seriously consider marrying, her brother, Rashid had disgraced their family. This meant the family of the man in question refused to give their permission to the marriage. If truth be known Zhora was relieved.

The actions of her brother had had a serious effect on both parents, causing her mother to have some form of breakdown, and her poor father to eventually suffer a heart attack. Zhora was called upon to stay at home and nurse them both. This she faithfully did, until her father passed away and her younger brother had moved his young wife and child into the family home. The memories were painful.

Sighing, Zhora put the card in her bag, cleared her mind, and set to dedicating herself to the afternoon.

ZHORA

About the Reunion…

That evening when she arrived home, having had a good afternoon, Zhora was feeling relaxed and content. Entering the house, she could smell the aroma of cooking coming from the kitchen.

"Hello, darling," said Ray from the kitchen doorway. "You okay."

Smiling at him, she said, "Yes, I feel good. And I'm hungry. Something smells delicious." And she kissed him warmly to show her appreciation.

"Mmm… Nice," he said, enjoying the taste of his wife. "Go and change, dinner will be ready in ten minutes," and he returned to the kitchen.

Later, having eaten and washed up, the couple sat on the couch in their lounge. Zhora finally told Ray about the morning's upset. He was, as always, very understanding, understanding that the bust-up was probably long overdue. The one thing he had never done was interfere where his wife's family was concerned, even though it took lots of self-control sometimes for him not to say anything at all.

Suddenly Zhora jumped up and going into the hall she plucked the pink envelope from her bag, returning to the lounge waving it in the air.

"What you got there, honey?" asked Ray.

"It's an invitation to a class reunion. It came to moms this morning, addressed to me in my maiden name," she announced opening the envelope to show him the invitation card.

She then began telling Ray all about the girls she had known at school, and how they had made those years fun, interesting and enjoyable. She hadn't realised, up until receiving the invitation, how much she had missed them all and those days.

"So, what do you think, Ray? Should we go?"

Ray looked at the card. "Yes, I think we should. It will do you good, and you will enjoy meeting your old friends again. But, you think about it. Your decision."

Allowing his wife some time to think about the invitation, he finally asked, "So! Are we going to go to the reunion?"

Looking at him Zhora smiled. "Yes, we are. Besides, I have a very handsome husband to show off, don't I," and she laughed as he swept her into his arms and kissed her soundly.

LORRAINE

On the job...

For the first time in her career, Lorraine was feeling apprehensive. Or maybe she was afraid. The decisions she made today could affect several people. Some good, some bad.

"What do you think, Gov?" asked her second-in-command, "Do we go in now, or wait a bit longer?"

Lorraine didn't respond immediately. She needed some time to consider the outcome of either action. Finally, she said, "Give it another ten minutes, Smithy, then we go in!"

Smithy nodded his head. If he was honest and had been asked, he would have agreed with his governor. Another ten minutes could mean the difference between life and death. Suddenly the portable phone began ringing.

Smithy snatched the receiver up and in a gruff dry voice said, "Yes; what can we do for you?" After listening for a minute or two he placed his hand over the mouthpiece and turning to his boss said, "He wants to talk, Gov. He's ready to let the hostages go and will give himself up if you guarantee his safety. What shall I tell him?"

Lorraine thought for a few seconds then taking the phone from Smithy she spoke into it. "Chief Inspector Watson here. Okay, Granville, I agree, but… you have to let the kids go now. Open the door and let them come out. Any nonsense and it will go bad for you later."

She listened for a few seconds before replacing the receiver then turning to Smithy said, "Tell the officers he's letting the hostages out; then he'll give himself up. AND… if anyone does anything wrong or puts their hands on him in the wrong way, they'll have me to answer to, okay?"

"Yes Gov," responded Smithy, breathing a sigh of relief at the result.

Ten minutes later, with the hostages being whisked away to the hospital to be checked over, Granville came out with his hands in the air. Once the officers saw he was unarmed they swooped in, capturing him and, not too gently, throwing him to the ground. Lorraine was immediately at the scene, issuing instructions in a clear and strong voice.

Finally face to face with the villain, she said, "Good move, Granville. You wouldn't have wanted to harm your children, now would you?"

The man didn't respond. He just hung his head in shame at what he had almost done.

* * * * *

An hour later, Lorraine was sitting at the desk in her office thinking, 'Maybe it's time you got out of this Lori. Time to retire.'

A knock at the door disturbed her thoughts. She called out, "Enter."

Smithy popped his head around the door of the room, asking, "You okay Gov?"

She smiled at the man. "Sure, Smithy. Just a little tired. It's been a long day. Time to go home I think."

Smithy nodded his head in agreement, then wishing her a goodnight he left the room. Twenty minutes later, Lori left as well, wishing the Desk Sergeant a goodnight as she departed.

LORRAINE

Unexpected desertion…

Making her way home, Lorraine once more reviewed the day's events. These hostage situations were becoming more regular, and increasingly more stressful. Maybe next time she would get a negotiator in. She had only taken charge this time because she knew Granville of old, having dealt with him many times over the years since she was a copper on the beat. He was a troubled soul who had had a rough lifestyle. Bad parents, nicked for petty shoplifting more than once, and one long stretch for driving the getaway car in a botched bank holdup. 'Mixing with the wrong crowd,' was how the Judge had summoned it up in court, giving him a lesser sentence as he hadn't done anything other than sit in the car.

Being a police officer wasn't easy but it was Lorraine's life. She had always known that she was destined to join the police force. It was a job she enjoyed doing.

Pulling into the driveway of her semi-detached house, Lorraine was both relieved and disappointed to see that the house lights were out. That meant Mark wasn't at home so she would have a peaceful evening.

Entering the house Lori heard the mewing of the cat. Going through to the kitchen she said, "Hello puss. How are you? Are you hungry?" The cat was a blue Persian and upon seeing her mistress she brushed herself up against Lori's legs. Bending down to stroke the cat she said, "Has no one fed you puss?" Going to the cupboard she took a sachet of cat food and filled the cat's dishes. One with food, the other with fresh milk.

Leaving the cat to eat, Lori went upstairs to change out of her uniform. As she entered her bedroom she stopped aghast at the mess.

"What the hell," she said out loud.

Everywhere she looked there were clothes thrown about. Mainly hers. The drawers were wide open with things hanging out or lying on the floor beneath. Looking around the room she noted the wardrobe doors were flung open. Going to inspect, she noted the space on the hanging rail and the shelves where her fiancé's clothes had once been. Searching further, Lori found that her boyfriend's belongings, normally kept in the drawers, were now gone. Slowly, it dawned on her - he had finally packed and left. For a moment she felt nothing but relief. At last, she was rid of him.

Sitting on the edge of the bed Lori thought back to their last conversation that morning. "What time will you be home tonight?" Mark had asked.

Looking up from the breakfast table she had thought first before responding, "Probably about seven, depending on how the day goes. What about you? Will you be here? Shall I bring a takeaway back with me?"

"No need, I'll not be here." He had said no more. And Lori hadn't questioned him further.

As she looked around the bedroom once more, it dawned on her that she should have been more aware, perhaps known what he had planned. 'Oh well,' she thought and began changing out of her uniform.

Once dressed, she began sorting out the mess on display before her. She started by hanging up the clothes thrown on the floor, then turned her attention to the drawers. As she began replacing and tidying those items tossed on the floor, it suddenly dawned on her that some things were missing. She thought they might have been pushed to the back of the drawers or were on the floor beneath the dropped items. However, once everything was back in its place, then and only then, did she suspect that she had been robbed!

"The bastard," she said loudly.

Mark had only gone and taken her jewellery. Not that she had much but what she had was quality stuff and worth a bob or two. Mark had taken most of it, leaving her with the cheaper dregs. But, if he'd taken the jewellery what else had disappeared?

Going to the cupboard in the corner she opened the door, discovering another mess inside. He'd gone through everything; perhaps looking for what else he could take.

The thing was, it was she who felt the fool in all this.

LORRAINE

Back in time…

Bending down she began picking up the items thrown so carelessly on the cupboard floor. The last thing she found thrown to one side was the Brampton School Year Book. As it happened, Mark had just tossed it away thinking it was of no importance.

Lorraine laughed. Had Mark thought to show more interest in it and look inside he would have been surprised to find a flat envelope. One in which he would most certainly have been interested.

Taking the book, she went to sit on the bed. Carefully opening the book at the rear, she removed the large envelope taped to the back page. Removing the contents, Lori checked that everything was still there – a substantial sum of money, the details of her bank accounts, plus the passwords, in code, as well as a Black Montblanc fountain pen. At least Mark hadn't taken these.

As she looked at the pen, memories of the day she had received it, flooded into her mind. It had been a leaving gift from Fran. One of the 'Musketeers.'

That's what all the girls in the netball team had been called at school. The name had stuck, but no one knew why, or why the teachers had first started calling the girls by the nickname. After all, there were seven of them, not the 'three-plus d'Artagnan' as portrayed in Dumas' book. Maybe it was because somehow, regardless of their different backgrounds, the girls had gelled as a team, and they had finally won the Inter-school Netball Competition in their final year at school.

Lorraine smiled to herself. She had enjoyed school, especially that last year, but had been sad to say goodbye to her soul mates.

At least that's what she had thought they were. Each had gone their separate ways and she was sorry that she hadn't kept in touch. However, having signed up to join the police force she had left home and gone to Hendon for training. By the time she returned home again, the girls had scattered to their various lifestyles.

Turning to the photograph of the netball team Lori studied each of the girls. How different we had all looked back then.

The question now though was what to do about Mark and the missing jewellery? It wouldn't exactly be amusing to have to go in to work tomorrow and report him for theft. In fact, it would be quite humiliating and would no doubt cause a big titter to go around the station when it was found that the boss had been ripped off. But then again, why should he be allowed to get away with it?

Mmmm… A difficult choice to make – be embarrassed or catch a thief. Perhaps that's what Mark is relying on? She would sleep on it and decide in the morning.

LORRAINE

A debt to pay…

The following morning as Lori was about to leave for work the postman called. Pushing the mail inside her briefcase she was about to lock up when she decided to leave the house by a different route. She had suddenly remembered that Mark only had the front door key and she hadn't seen it lying around, which mean he could still have it on him. Not wanting to run the risk of him returning while she was at work and removing other stuff she bolted the front door, then left by the back ensuring the alarm was properly set. At least he would have a problem getting back inside if that was his intention.

Arriving at work she was met by Smithy, her second in command.

"Morning Gov. Good result yesterday."

"It certainly was," replied Lori before continuing. "You got a minute, Smithy? I need to ask you something." Surprised by her request Smithy followed his boss into her room, closing the door shut behind him. It wasn't often she asked for his advice but when she did, he accepted that she valued his opinion.

Indicating that Smithy take a seat Lori took a moment or two before speaking. "Smithy, I've been robbed." Before he could react, she held her hand up to stop him from speaking. "What I am about to tell you is confidential, and in a lot of respects very embarrassing – to me."

Taking a breath she continued. "Mark has left me, and he's taken my jewellery. Whilst it's not worth a massive amount it is still valuable to me. The problem I have, is - if I make a report, I know it will go around the station like wildfire and I'll become a laughing stock. To be honest that's the last thing I need right now. However, the police officer in me doesn't want him to get away with it. So, as a friend and a fellow officer, I am asking if you have any suggestions?"

Smithy didn't respond immediately. Finally, he said, "I see the problem, Gov, and I suppose I have to agree. In reality, you cannot let him get away with it. Mmm… Tell you what, why don't you let me handle it. I'll err… make a few inquiries and see what I can find out. If I find him, I'll have a quiet word and suggest he returns the stuff. That is if he hasn't sold it already. Any clues as to where he might have gone?"

Thinking it over, all Lori could do was suggest Mark's sister, or his best friend Jay. With the information, Smithy left the room. After he had gone

Lori relaxed. If there was one thing Lori knew, it was that she could trust Smithy to be discrete.

After Smithy had gone Lori opened her briefcase and took out the mail she had dropped inside. Apart from the usual bills, she discovered the pink envelope addressed to her at home which her father must have forwarded to her. Tearing it open, Lori was surprised to discover the invitation to the school reunion.

'How strange,' she thought, especially as she had only been thinking about the girls the night before. The only question now was should she go? Perhaps she'd sleep on the idea for a day or two before making her decision.

* * * * *

Two days later, Smithy knocked on her office door. "Got a minute, Gov?"

Waving him inside, she pointed to a seat, before asking him what she could do for him.

Smiling, he held up a coloured plastic shopping bag. "I think these are yours, Gov?"

Taking the bag, Lori slowly opened it. Inside was her camera, an old mobile phone, a pair of small ornate Wedgwood vases, and at the bottom a small plastic bag with her jewellery inside. Looking up surprise showed on her face.

"You found him and got my stuff back? How?"

Smithy smiled. "Easy. I told him, that despite

187

him thinking you wouldn't do anything, if he didn't give back everything he had stolen from you, including the door key, you would, without hesitation throw the book at him. I also told him you would also humiliate double the humiliation and embarrassment that you received by having to report the theft. I further told him that once he was prosecuted and locked up, I would make it my life's mission to ensure he had a very unhappy life. Err... sorry, Gov, but I needed to call his bluff. He genuinely thought you wouldn't do anything so I think he was a little shocked, but he still tried to call my bluff. Anyway, I think everything is there. If you can check it, please?"

Lori sat back in her chair, looking at Smithy with new respect. "I don't know what to say, or how to repay you for doing this. What can I do?"

"Nothing, Gov. I'm pleased I could help," and Smithy stood up, ready to leave.

As he reached the door, Lori suddenly did something unexpected, which shocked both her and Smithy. "Smithy. Err... you're single, right? No girlfriend at the moment?"

Laughing, Smithy said, "Yes, Gov and No... no girlfriend. We broke up about two months ago. Hard to keep a girl when you're in the job."

Swallowing, Lori took a deep breath. "Smithy, this is going to sound a bit peculiar but... err... I've received an invitation to attend a school reunion. It's on the first of August. It says I can take A. N. other person and err… well, I wondered if you fancied a night out. On me."

Silenced descended on the room as the pair looked at each other. Then shaking her head, Lori, said, "Sorry. That was a stupid thing to say, wasn't it? Forget it."

Smithy crossed the room and bending over he placed his hands on her desk. Looking her in the eyes, he said, "Actually, Lorraine, I would very much like to have a night out with you, if the offer stills stand."

Silence reined for seconds until finally Lori nodded her head, and said, "Great. I'm not sure what it will be like but it saves me going in my uniform," and she laughed. "I'll let you have the details later, okay."

Straightening, Smithy smiled, saying, "Perfectly okay, Gov," then turning he left the room.

After he had gone Lori could not believe what she had just done. Smithy was her second in command and she had just propositioned him into going on a date with her.

'My God,' she thought. 'I must be mad.' But then she thought about his eyes staring into hers and thought, 'Why not. I'm a free agent now. Mmm… this could prove interesting."

* * * * *

That evening at home, Lori responded to the invitation to the reunion, informing the organiser that she would be attending with a friend. She did rethink about whether or not to turn up in her uniform. The idea made her laugh, as she imagined the look of shock on people's faces. Not to mention poor Smithy's.

Thinking about Smithy she realised how different he was from her ex-fiancée. That relationship had gone sour months ago. The only problem, she thought there could be, was the fact that Smithy was younger than her. Younger by nearly ten years. She must be mad to have asked him to go with her. But she couldn't back out now. It wouldn't be fair. And he had got all her belongings back for her, hadn't he?

'No, I'd better not back out. A date with Smithy it is. Looks like I'm going to have to buy a new dress, after all, I'll need to make an effort, at least for one night.'

Little did Lori realise what a night it would turn out to be, or how it would change her future life.

SUSIE

When life turns sour…

The weekend had dragged on and on and, for the first time in years, Susie realised how quiet the house was. Up to now, she'd never noticed that. Wandering around the large detached house that was her home she began opening cupboards and drawers; starting with the large wardrobe that housed her husband's clothes. Quickly she shut it. The pain was still too much for her to bear. Besides, she wasn't ready yet to face the reality of that place.

Turning towards the small store cupboard in the corner she opened the door to survey what was enclosed within there. Scanning the shelves her eyes settled on the title of an old book – Class of '64 was printed on the binder. Reaching out she grabbed the book, then closing the door she turned and went downstairs to the kitchen for a cup of tea.

Sitting at the table, Susie slowly turned the pages of her old school yearbook. Her eyes ran over the faces of the girls from the netball team; those she had played alongside. The photographs stirred vibrant memories of that last day at school.

It had started the same as any other day with the

sound of the youngster's excited chatter and laughter being heard clear across the sun-filled playground. As they came nearer the school, the level of noise had increased, and upon entering the old building, the sound had seemed to bounce off the walls, echoing down the long corridors. That day no one had told them to be quiet, besides they weren't in any hurry to cease their incessant noise. Being the last day of term the teachers were inclined to be a little more relaxed, as the excitement of breaking up for the end of term seemed to be contagious. It was more so for them as it was their last day at the school before they stepped out into the big bad world!

Everyone had been looking forward to the last day. And whilst most were filled with anticipation of six weeks on holiday, some were tinged with sadness and just maybe, a smattering of regret that something wonderful was coming to an end. Despite all that, every pupil was happy that for the next few weeks they wouldn't have to rise early, eat a quick breakfast, or race to catch the school bus. And, of course, there would be no homework to do. From the next day onwards, they knew they could stay in bed, ignore the alarm clock, and best of all, they could stop wearing their horrible, green coloured school uniform. The next six weeks were going to be bliss! With a summer holiday in-between, it gave those returning something exciting to talk about before the dreaded new term started later in the year.

Susie remembered the feelings which had affected everyone. They had been both happy and sad moments. None more so than for the 'Musketeers.'

Suddenly, she smiled at the memories. The reference to the Musketeers had not been about those mythical heroes from French history. No, it referred to a group of young girls who, during their first year at the senior school, had been aptly nick-named this by their history teacher. Somehow, the girls involved in the merry band had found their way into each other's company; discovering a common bond that would strengthen and continue. At least until that very last day. Although it had been a joyous time for their group, the day had also been filled with sorrow. Slowly it dawned on each girl that when the final bell rang, they would leave the historical old building, and probably each other as they each went their separate ways.

'What promises we had made,' thought Susie. 'How we were going to keep in touch; to see each other as much as possible!' She sighed, wondering what had gone wrong? Had any of them even tried to keep those promises? Perhaps not. She knew she hadn't tried.

Closing the book, she picked up the cold cup of tea and threw the contents down the sink. After washing the cup, she flicked the switch on the kettle and made a fresh brew. That's all she seemed to do these days; make tea, let it go cold, throw it away, and then make a fresh one which she also didn't drink. She sighed once more, a sense of sadness enveloping her. But not just at the loss of her close school friends.

SUSIE

Organising the event...

Hearing the rattle of the letterbox Susie left the kitchen to fetch the mail which had just dropped onto the hall floor behind the door. Shuffling back down the hall she stopped in front of the mirror. Looking at her reflection, she wondered for a moment if that was herself staring back at her.

Staring at her image, she thought, 'I look a mess.'

Suddenly the silence of the hallway was shattered by the sound of the telephone blaring out. It caused her to jump. It hadn't stopped ringing all morning; she decided to ignore it. The last call had been the caterers for the reunion, pressing her for the final numbers. They hadn't sounded too pleased when she had reminded them that there were at least another six days to go before they needed the final figures.

'Only ten more days,' she thought, 'what on earth had possessed me to consider organising such an event? I must have been mad!'

She had managed to post all the pink envelopes containing the invitations about five weeks ago. There had been forty in all. The message inside had read the same, although it had probably been received differently by each recipient. Six girls, in particular, had been of more concern to Susie. As she had finished writing the name and address for each of those six, she had turned the envelope over and written the word 'Musketeer!' on the back.

It was only then that Susie had remembered how the seven of them had met. It had been in their first year of senior school, each radiating towards the others after discovering common ground in the sport of netball. They had melded together like Dumas' heroes, whom they had been studying at the time. Although there were more than the usual three, the girls had gelled together, being given the nickname, the Musketeers, sometime during that first year. It had stuck.

Over time most of the teachers began referring to the merry band of girls by this name. Not that they had minded as they felt it made them extra special. Eventually, the group took up Dumas's warriors' infamous cry - 'All for one; one for all' - especially when playing sport. Being on the netball team meant their friendship continued throughout the whole of their senior years, remaining strong, until that very last school day. And yet, despite their promises and vows of eternal devotion, each had gone their separate way; quickly losing contact with the others.

And now here she was, trying to bring them back

together. Well, not just them but all the class of 64. Again, she questioned her sense in doing this. What had she been thinking of by agreeing to organise the reunion, especially with all the other things happening in her life? She supposed it had seemed a good idea at the time. Something to keep her occupied, stop her moping or worrying. And in some ways, it had!

SUSIE

Life is unfair…

Guiltily, it suddenly dawned on Susie that she hadn't thought about Ted in days, or at least not that much. Ted, her one true love, the centre of her world, who was now gone! She supposed his desertion had, in reality, not been unexpected. That much was true. But still, it had come as a big shock that morning when she had woken to find him gone, with only a short note left lying on the pillow, telling her of his decision.

He had written how he was sorry and hoped that she would, in time, understand. He was gone. Never to return. She had kept the note. A reminder of the treachery of the only man she had ever loved.

Ted or Edward Smith had been in the same year as Susie. He had been comical, often being disruptive in class. His best friend had been Tommy Richardson, although he had left school 'under a dark cloud' before the end of that last year. Like most of the girls, Susie had liked Ted. Having had a crush on him for some time. He had been tall and good-looking, with a lovely smile that you couldn't help but respond to.

Suddenly, Susie smiled to herself as she remembered that smile. It had caused his blue eyes to twinkle and gleam. During the last few weeks of term the two of them had started talking, until finally, Ted had asked her to go to the school prom with him. She had been delighted, knowing she would be the envy of all the other girls.

After they had left school, she and Ted had kept in touch, often seeing each other in the local café or the pictures. About four months later he had asked Susie to go steady. Within eighteen months the pair were married; much to her mother's disgust. Mind you, under the circumstances, her mother had to agree to the wedding as Debbie was born seven months later.

Her father had at first been filled with disappointment meaning only Justin her brother had supported her through that time but eventually her dad had come round and they had remained friends until he left for the Bahamas.

Even though the young couple had been forced to get married they were, for the most part, happy and well suited to each other. This state of affairs had lasted for many years, with Susie believing she had found her soul mate for life.

Surfacing back to the present Susie found tears slowly rolling down her face. Sobbing she stared at the photograph of her husband hung on the hall wall, declaring out loudly, "Oh my God, what am I going to do without you, Ted?   Why did you have to leave me like this? Why? Why? Why?"

Having sobbed uncontrollably for some minutes, Susie finally dried her eyes, then taking a deep breath, she calmed herself. 'Life is so unfair,' she thought, 'so unfair.'

SUSIE

Memories hurt but…

Suddenly the phone started ringing again. Pulling herself together she went to answer it.

"Susie Smith," she said, hoping she sounded normal and calm. "Yes," she said listening, "I am the person organising the Class of '64 Reunion… No… it is free to Old Brampton School pupils. How can I help you?"

There followed a short pause while she listened to the caller talking, made notes on the pad by the phone, then completing the call she replaced the receiver on the cradle. That's another two people, she noted. With the number of RSVPs coming in, it was going to be a great party after all. Picking up the note and the post, she returned to the kitchen where she dropped the pile of mail on the table while she went to make herself yet another fresh cuppa.

Sitting down at the table, Susie picked up the post and slowly sorted it into piles. There was quite a lot. Those that appeared to contain larger cards she put to one side. She would read those with her daughter Debbie when she came home later. At this moment in time, she still couldn't read them on her own. The hardest part was reading the nice sentiments people had written. Some shared their memories of Ted from years past. Others didn't know what to say but had taken care with the card they had chosen, usually picking one with a nice verse full of comforting platitudes. If they only knew that all the nice words in the world couldn't take away the pain and the awful emptiness inside her.

The phone rang again. Tempted as she was to ignore it, she thought better of the idea as it would probably be her step-sister. Quickly she made her way to the hall, but by the time Susie picked the receiver up the caller had hung up. 'Oh well,' she thought. 'Whoever it is will no doubt ring back.'

Thinking about her step-sister, Susie had to admit that at first, she had been surprised that her sibling had taken to ringing her nearly every day. Always asking if she and Debbie were okay. 'More likely to see if I'm coping or not,' Susie thought, making her way back to the kitchen, 'and no doubt to gloat. She'd never really liked Ted anyway.'

Sometimes Susie wanted to shout and scream out loud. 'No, I'm not coping – why should I, it's not fair; my husband isn't here anymore. He ran away with someone else.' But she rarely thought about that part of her loss. Yet it was true. Ted had left her for someone else. But not for some strange woman; oh no. It was worse than that. He had left her for another man.

Now, how cruel was that?

It wasn't that Susie was homophobic. 'After all, each to their own,' she thought. But his desertion had been like a blow to the very core of her being. Did his change of sexual allegiance mean that their whole life together had been one big lie? 'Did he know he was gay?' thought Susie. 'If so, why didn't he confess sooner instead of letting me continue to believe that everything was okay with our marriage?'

And that was the hardest part. Discovering that the man she had loved so deeply wasn't who he pretended to be. That he loved someone else more than her. Then to cap it all off, he had gone and got himself killed whilst on his way to meet his lover.

A bad car accident, the Police had told her. 'Wrong place, wrong time, Ted,' she thought, grimacing to herself.

Passing the lounge on her way back to the kitchen, Susie looked at the cards spread all around. To no one, in particular, she shouted out loud, "You all thought Ted was the salt of the earth. Oh, if you'd only known the truth. Would you still have written your words of comfort...? I think not."

Surprising herself by her reaction she shook her head. "Hell! What am I doing, ranting at a shelf full of sympathy cards? I must be going nuts! Come on girl, get a grip and stop feeling sorry for yourself."

Returning to the kitchen she picked up the rest of the post, finished opening the response cards to the invitations, and ticked the names off the list she had made as she read each one. It now totalled 35 old boys and girls. With the partners, the overall total would be 60 people and there were still five days to go for replies. She looked at the names again, noting that at least ten of the people who were going to be attending would be single.

'Well, at least I won't be the only one,' she thought sarcastically.

The telephone started to ring again so she went to answer it. Looking at her watch she thought it might be her step-sister, and whilst tempted to ignore it, she knew that wouldn't be nice of her. Anyway, if she did that, she would have to make an excuse the next time she spoke to her and Susie didn't want to start lying to her sibling after she had been so supportive over the last few weeks.

Picking up the receiver she was about to say hello, but before she did her daughter's voice came on the line.

"Hi Mom," Debbie said, "Are you okay?"

Susie started to panic, quickly asking her daughter what was wrong.

"Nothing Mom," replied Debbie. "I just wanted to check that you were okay and to say, if you want me to, I think I would like to go to the reunion with you after all if that's okay?"

Susie breathed a sigh of relief. Smiling she replied, "Of course, Darling. That's wonderful… Let's talk about it when you get home. And Debbie… I love you. See you later. Bye," and she hung up the phone.

Turning to go back into the kitchen, Susie again caught sight of her reflection in the hall mirror, this time noticing that she was smiling. Gently stroking the hair which had fallen over her face, she took another look at the picture of her husband, saying out loud, "At least something good came from our marriage, Ted. Our beautiful daughter!"

THE REUNION

"Don't worry Mom," Debbie whispered in Susie's ear, "Everything is going to be perfect. You look lovely."

"Do you think so?" Susie whispered back. Debbie smiled, nodding her head in agreement.

As the day of the reunion had drawn ever closer, Susie had grown more and more nervous. She had started worrying about the event, whether it would be a success or not. With everything that was happening in her life at the moment, she was hoping that she hadn't forgotten anything. And now, with the time of the event being here and the people starting to arrive, it was making her even more nervous.

Being the hostess, Susie knew she had to forget her fears and take control, making sure she welcomed as many of those arriving as she could. Thinking about it, what excited her most about tonight was the thought of meeting her six teammates again. Even after all the time that had passed.

'They were good friends,' she thought. 'Weren't they?' She hesitated, then told herself, 'Of course, they were.' She was trying to reassure herself. 'Oh, if only they would arrive.'

The reception area for the event had been set up outside the large room where the reunion was taking place. Susie had decorated the room with a big banner declaring - 'Old Brampton Reunion.' There were also some enlarged school photos pinned up around the walls. As people recognised themselves, they laughed out loud at how quirky they had looked back then.

* * * * *

"Melinda, Melinda Jones. Is that you?" asked a voice enquiringly. Melinda, turning around wondered where the soft Irish voice had come from.

"Down here girl," stated the voice, seeing that Melinda, who was extremely tall, was looking over her head.

Melinda dropped her gaze. "Coleen! You're... you're in a wheelchair," she exclaimed, a look of pure shock on her face.

"Yes!" responded Coleen laughingly, "and you're at least four feet taller than I remember. How are you, Melinda?"

"Oh, I am so happy to see you," she replied as she bent to kiss her school friend on the cheek. "Come on, let's go get a drink. We can sit over there," and she pointed to a set of tables and chairs in the far corner of the room.

Collecting drinks for them both, Melinda joined Coleen at the table, and from that moment on it was as if the two had never been apart. Soon they were chatting away to each other, and it was as if time had never passed them by.

* * * * *

A short time later, Fran quite literally marched into the room.

She hadn't worn high heels for a very long time and, if she were honest, she was still finding it a little difficult to walk in a ladylike way. She had practised walking around the house in the shoes until she felt easier wearing them. The new outfit she had bought in the high street whilst out shopping with her mother, suited her perfectly. However, Fran, still feeling a little nervous at being in civvies, had dressed with care.

Stopping in the doorway she slowly surveyed the room, looking for a familiar face. As Fran's eyes wandered around the room they settled on the seats where she caught sight of Coleen and Melinda sitting at one of the tables. Carefully she strode across the room to join them. The two girls were delighted to see her.

* * * * *

Susie, who had been kept quite busy greeting people, and explaining where everything was, hadn't noticed the three girls sitting in the corner of the room. As she headed towards the entrance she stopped, suddenly recognising the woman standing in the doorway.

"Phillipa," she enquired. "Is that you, Phillipa?"

"Susie," said Phillipa warmly. "It is you. Oh, it's

so nice to see you again. Meet my husband, Roland."

Then moving to the side she introduced her husband, allowing Susie the opportunity to shake hands with Roland, before smartly sending him off to get them both something to drink.

Ever since the weekend of the phone call Roland had been more attentive toward his wife. And though he was reluctant in wanting to be at the reunion, he now knew better than to argue with Phillipa. To him, it was as if she had found a new view on the way she wanted their or at least her life to go. Until he was sure she didn't know anything about his extra-marital affairs he needed to keep her happy. Little did he realise exactly what she did know, but that is for another time.

Having been chatting with Phillipa for a few moments, Susie found herself distracted by some new arrivals so having to make her excuses she left to greet them.

Left alone, Phillipa began searching the room. Suddenly her eyes fell on the three girls sitting in the corner so she decided to make a bee-line towards them. Without a moment's hesitation, or waiting for Roland to rejoin her, she headed off across the room. Greeting them warmly. It was as if the girls had never been apart, with the years slipping away. Soon they all started giggling and talking at once.

* * * * *

It was about ten minutes later, Zhora and Ray standing in the doorway, surveyed the room. Despite having her husband by her side Zhora was still feeling a little nervous. Slowly, she searched the room, finally spotting some of her special friends huddled together in a corner, all laughing out loud. Pointing towards the corner she told Ray she had found four of her friends.

Seeing her smile, he kissed her on the cheek, saying, "Off you go then, go on... off you go. I'll go get us a drink and give you time to catch up." And before she could respond he had quickly turned and disappeared towards the bar, leaving her with no option but to walk across to join the four women.

"Hello," said Zhora timidly, wary of how they would react, and whether or not they would even recognise her. However, she need not have worried, for in one chorus the four echoed her name:

"Zhora? Is it really you? You look gorgeous. We didn't know if you could come."

All at once, the years slipped away, and within seconds the five were chatting merrily, wanting to know what each other had been up to - whether they were married, did they have children, and what job they each had. The questions went on and on.

Ray and Roland, having met each other at the bar, finally approached the women, where each man was introduced to the ladies. The fact that Zhora had married an English man had certainly surprised the others although they were delighted when they saw how happy she looked. After that the poor men didn't get much of a look in so they quietly slipped away, returning to stand at the bar where they were joined in conversation by some of the other spouses who were also accompanying ex-pupils.

* * * * *

Not long afterwards, Lorraine stood in the doorway to the large room. Looking around she searched for any faces she recognised. Her eyes finally settled on the group of girls sitting in the corner. Could it be they were her teammates?

"So, Lori. What are you waiting for?" asked Smithy. "Are we going in or not?"

Turning towards Smithy, she replied, "I'm not sure this was a good idea."

"You're being silly. Come on, let's circulate," he answered, taking a reassuring grip on her arm. "You'll be fine. But first, what we need is a drink," upon which note Smithy steered her towards the bar. As they crossed the floor Lori saw the group in the corner looking at her.

Suddenly one of them stood up and crossed the room, calling out, "Lorraine, is that you?"

It was Melinda. "Wow, it's great to see you. Come and join us," she continued. And, before Lori knew what was happening, Melinda had put her arm around her friend, literally pulling her towards the corner table.

Once there she was quickly wrapped in the warmth of her friends' welcome, which is where Smithy found her. Knowing she had to introduce him she wasn't at first sure what to say.

Finally, she said, "This is Smithy, sorry Rob. He's a friend and a co-worker."

She shouldn't have been worried at the girls' response for they welcomed him warmly into the fold, after which he took the opportunity to disappear to the bar, joining Roland and Ray. The three men decided that it would be better to leave the ladies alone for now, allowing them time to catch up with each other.

* * * * *

Sometime later in the evening after her duties were over, Susie finally took more notice of the six women sitting in the corner. Secretly, she had been watching them from across the room, wanting to join in the fun they seemed to be having. But, she had been too nervous to go forward, thinking, 'Maybe we hadn't been friends after all. I know I must have been a bit a snob.' She found the idea upsetting.

As she was about to turn away, Melinda caught sight of her, and looking her straight in the eyes, she smiled. 'Are you free to join us now, Susie?' Melinda mouthed across the room. 'We want to hear all your news.'

Smiling back, Susie suddenly felt everything was going to be alright. They were her friends after all. Nodding, she quickly made her way across the room, soon finding herself welcomed into the middle of the group. Before long she was giggling and laughing like the schoolgirl she had once been.

Coleen suddenly said, "Hey girls, do you remember what they used to call us?"

Looking at each other they all smiled, then each raised an arm in the air, and 'as one, the seven girls sang out, "*All for One. And One for All*."

After which they literally collapsed in fits of laughter, making the other people in the room turn around and look at them smilingly, as they too remembered the famous cry of the Seven Brampton Musketeers.

Susie looked at her daughter, who had joined the group. She smiled, thinking, 'What a great reunion this has turned out to be. Everything will be alright now. I know it will.'

THE FUTURE

After the ball... I mean the reunion...

Unfortunately, we are not able to foresee or predict what our future will hold for us. We can only wish and work towards achieving the desires we wish for.

Zhora having decided her life was mapped out for her could say she was surprised that the man she thought she would marry wasn't the one she did.

Melinda's bad experience at the hands of her brother proved to not only lead her down the path of an unusual career but led her to a position in life not many from a poor background could hope to achieve.

The determination of Lorraine and Fran showed the strength of these two young women and hopefully, their lives would prove to grow as they changed their path of life.

Susie had it all while young but paid the ultimate price yet there was still hope for her. While Phillipa will not let life get her down no matter what.

This leaves Coleen, perhaps she is the one who has suffered the most and yet she could be the one who will outdo all the other six Musketeers when it comes to proving that life is still worth living regardless.

If it was left solely to us I am sure we would

love to be able to plan our life course, knowing that the journey along which we chose to travel would turn out the way we planned. Unfortunately, that isn't how it's always meant to be. Many other factors will interfere with that journey, and no matter how much one is determined to succeed it doesn't necessarily work out the way we want or believe it should.

At the end of the day, all people ever really desire is happiness, good health, and security. And we can only hope the same for the Brampton Musketeers and that they too will find that out for themselves.

In the meantime here's a little idea of how their future journey progressed but not necessarily ended…

MELINDA

Helping her friend...

Two weeks after the reunion, Coleen was shown into Melinda's lounge by the butler. As she wheeled herself in she looked around in awe. The place was amazing; the likes of which she had never seen before.

"Wow, Mel, what a place you have. How on earth did you manage to get this? Sorry, I shouldn't ask should I," and Coleen giggled.

Deciding to be a bit cheeky, and trying to shock Coleen, Melinda quietly replied, "I opened my legs wide, enough times!"

Coleen, looking at Melinda, had shock written across her face. "You did what?"

Laughing, Mel sat next to Coleen, saying, "I was a call girl. A very high-class prostitute. Then I met Simon, Lord Priestly-Teddington, while on the game. We fell in love, so I became his trophy girlfriend. Eventually, he asked me to give up the game and live with him. Finally, we married."

As Mel had told her story, Coleen's mouth had slowly opened, wider and wider, and her eyes were ready to pop out of her face. "You are joking!"

"No. I'm serious. I still own a special kind of club – you could call it an up-market brothel in a very select part of London. Really. I mean it."

All Coleen could say was, "WOW!"

Melinda laughed lightly. "So, how long are staying in England?"

"I'm not sure. I suppose I'll have to go home sometime but to be honest I'm trying to put it off for as long as I can. My brother didn't want me to come over. Me being in a wheelchair and all that. But, I so wanted to see the girls…" and her voice trailed off.

The two ladies began talking about the past. Coleen told Melinda what had happened to her and how she had ended up in the wheelchair.

Melinda reciprocated by telling Coleen about how she had become one of the most exclusive call girls on the London prostitute scene. Coleen already knew about what her brother and his friend had done to her, as her aunt had helped Melinda after the event. Mel also explained more about meeting and marrying her late husband Simon.

Over the next few days, Coleen and Melinda spent a lot of time together, with Coleen asking more questions about why and how Melinda could have done what she had done. It was at this point that Melinda told her all the details about the rape by Tom and her brother not long before she left school.

"It wasn't, Tommy Edwards was it?" asked Coleen.

Laughing, Melinda said, "Hell, no. Tommy Wilkins. He was my brothers' friend. My brother had started messing about with me. Touching me up and all. Then one day, our parents left us alone overnight. Tom came to watch tv and they ganged up on me. They tied me to the bed and Tom raped me, then my brother had sex with me while I was still tied up."

Shocked, Coleen, asked, "You never rang the police did you?"

Melinda paused before answering. "No. To be honest I was frightened. But as my brother had been feeling me up for over a year I didn't think they would believe me. I was lucky I didn't get pregnant. Not that I would have as I can't have kids anyway."

"What! Oh, Mel, I'm so sorry. That is so unfair."

"It proved to be an advantage. When I left and went to stay with my aunt in London, it was she who got me on the game. I knew I couldn't get pregnant no matter how many men I had. My aunt was a madame. She said not being able to have kids would make me a fortune. And she was right. I am rolling in it. Not just from the club but from all I inherited from Simon. I suppose I can't complain, can I?"

Coleen sat looking at Melinda. She was amazed at how mature and strong she was, wishing she could be half as strong as her.

"What you thinking?" Melinda asked.

Smiling, Coleen said, "How I wish I could be a little bit like you. Strong and mature in your outlook."

"But you can, Col, you know you can."

"How? Look at me? If you hadn't noticed I'm stuck in a bloody wheelchair."

Melinda thought for a moment. Then she took a chance and asked, "Coleen, have you ever had sex?"

Surprised, Coleen couldn't stop herself from blushing. Shaking her head, she lowered her head. "I never got the chance. Not sure anyone would want me now, would they?"

Taking a deep breath Melinda said, "Actually, I know quite a few men who would want you."

Coleen didn't know what to say. Luckily at that moment the butler entered announcing that there was an important phone call for Melinda. Leaving the room, Coleen was left with her thoughts.

* * * * *

As Melinda hung up the phone she took a moment to think. The call had been 'a rave from the grave' and had left her unsure what to do next.

For a start, she needed to think about the conversation she had just had. But first, though she needed to go back to Coleen. What she had in mind for her would probably end their new-found friendship. Whilst it may come as a shock to her if Coleen was game, Melinda knew the perfect solution to Coleen's problem of not returning to Ireland.

'Mmmm…," she thought, "only time will tell.'

MELINDA

A pleasant lunch…

Arriving at the restaurant early, Melinda looked around. She knew she would recognise him and there he was sitting at a table in the corner. He looked up, catching her eye. They stared at one another.

"Can I help you, Madame," asked the waiter.

"I'm meeting a friend. That's him sat over there," and she pointed to the table.

Looking to where she pointed, the waiter said, "Follow me, please."

As they walked through the restaurant to the table, the customers already there, surreptitiously followed Melinda with their eyes. She walked with her head held high. She knew what some of them thought of her. A loose, younger woman married to a rich older man who dies within a year leaving her very well off. Little did they know she was wealthy in her own right long before she married Simon.

Arriving at the table she held out her hand and the man standing waiting for her took it into his hand and raising it to his lips he kissed it.

"Mon Cheri. Tu es toujours aussi belle (*you are as beautiful as ever*)." Then indicating the chair, he waited while she sat.

Melinda looked into the Baron's eyes. They were as beautiful a blue as they had ever been. "And how are you, Édouard? It's been a very long time."

"It is as if it was only yesterday," he replied with a strong French accent. "And I am as madly in love with you today as I have always been."

Melinda laughed, as under her breath she said, "Bullshit. The only person you have ever loved my dear Édouard is yourself."

The Baron, pulling a fake look of hurt across his face, said, "Mon Cheri, you cut me deeply."

They both laughed. "How are you, Édouard? I must say for a man of sixty you are looking extremely well. How's the wife?"

"Sadly, Mon Cheri, she has left me. Gone to join her son in the great sky above. Or maybe she's gone to hell. Either way, you see before you a windowed man. A very lonely widowed man!"

"And so you thought you would look an old friend up. For old times' sake perhaps?"

He nodded, taking a drink of the champagne he had ordered for them. "I see you are no longer at the club?"

"No," she replied, which wasn't quite true as she had been visiting and working on and off since six months after Simon's death. It had been the loneliness of the house, and the lack of male company in her bed which had driven her to occasionally look for companionship and sexual satisfaction.

"I do, however, still own it, which I presume is how you got my contact details."

He nodded to acknowledge that she was correct.

"So, Édouard," she asked, "what exactly is it that you want."

"Let's eat, and then go somewhere more conducive for a quiet intimate talk. I promise to tell you all then."

Despite her reluctance and impatience to know what Édouard wanted, Melinda decided to wait.

Maybe the afternoon would turn out to be more interesting than she had expected it to be.

MELINDA

Another new life…

Stretching, Melinda, cursed herself for having given in so easily. Hell, Édouard still had the gift of the gab as, having returned to her apartment, he had managed to talk his way into her knickers and her bed. It had been a long time since he had made love to her. Reluctantly she admitted having enjoyed every little minute.

"Okay, Édouard, own up. What is it you want?" she asked. He didn't answer immediately, being preoccupied with nibbling her neck. "Édouard, behave yourself and answer me… pleaseeee…"

Stopping what he was doing he, looked at her. "But, I am enjoying myself, Mon Cheri, and so are you."

Very sternly she said, "Édouard!"

Sitting up, Édouard smiled, saying, "Okay, Melinda, okay. What I want… is to… marry you. That is why I have come back."

The unexpected reason left Melinda shocked. Édouard had once been a part of her life, long before she met and fell in love with Simon. If truth be told he had been her first and only other love. But Édouard had been married, so she knew he was not free and he would never leave his wife. The family was old-school

French and divorce would not be accepted. Affairs yes, but divorce – never.

"So, my Mon Cheri, what do you say? Will you marry me? I have waited a long time for you. Please say yes?"

"Wow, Édouard, you certainly know how to floor a girl, don't you. Why now, after all this time?"

"Melinda, I loved you the moment I met you. But, I could not have you as I was married. You wouldn't agree to come and live in France and be my mistress, so I returned home broken-hearted. Now I am free, so I have come back for you. Say you will marry me, Melinda?"

After a long period of silence, Melinda said, "Édouard, a lot of water has flowed under the bridge since we last met. I have lived the life of a call girl; ok a high-end call girl, but I have still known many men. After you left I was deeply hurt but I knew you would never divorce your wife. Then I met Simon. I gave up that life for him, living with him until we married. He died less than a year ago. It is too soon yet for me to remarry. Even if I agreed to marry you, you will have to live with the knowledge of what I have done, who I have been. What about your children? What if your neighbours, the people you mix with, find out about me, it won't make for an easy life for you? Please consider fully what you are asking?"

The baron looked deflated. As if the bottom had fallen from his world. "I will not stop loving you. I also don't care about my neighbours. I will move if they annoy me. As for my children? If they cannot accept the woman I love, then I will denounce them. But, as you have requested I will consider my request. I will go away and I will come back with answers to show you that marrying me is the best thing you can do. Remember, Mon Cheri, I love you and that is all that matters." Then leaving the bed he got dressed and left the apartment.

* * * * *

True to his word the Baron thought long and hard about his desire to marry Melinda. He spoke to his children, being openly honest with them. Strangely, they agreed with him marrying Melinda. His eldest son had known about her, having been introduced to her on his twenty-first birthday.

Melinda had found a woman for the son and he had spent a marvellous night at the club. A gift from his father. This had created a bond between father and son. He wasn't worried that Melinda would take the family fortune. She was already rich, and he was now in control of the estate he would inherit on his father's death. The remainder of the children were already provided for under both French law and their father's Will.

Three months later he returned to London and seriously began courting Melinda. They became lovers from that moment on and were married in the family church in France four months later. All the children were present, as were the other Musketeers.

The Baron and Baroness Édouard Fitzherbert both lived a contented and happy life in a large house in a select part of London. They visited the Baron's French estate often, with Melinda soon being accepted by one and all.

PHILLIPA

A plan of action…

The reunion had brought a lot of memories back for Phillipa. Some were good, some not so. But it had also brought her to her senses. She had finally realised that she was being taken for a fool. Up to now, even though she had thought Roland was cheating she had still been unsure. The problem was, if he was cheating, then how to prove it. He was a smooth talker and quite slick in his actions. Plus, he could pull the wool over the eyes of anyone. Hell, he'd been doing with her for years now. Maybe now was the time to start taking some action. After all, she needed to secure her, and the boys, future.

* * * * *

Two weeks later, Phillipa arrived at the coffee shop for a meeting she had arranged to have with Lorraine. She wanted to ask Lori her professional opinion about what to do over her husband's behaviour.

"I know it's not your line of work, Lori," she said, "but, you do understand the law better than I do, so maybe you can advise me on what I can do to protect me and the boys?"

Lorraine felt sympathy for her friend, but she was right it wasn't her line of work. Still, if she could, she would try to help her as Phillipa looked worn down by the whole affair. Besides, she had met Roland Fitzpatrick and she knew a creep when she met one. He was certainly a smooth-talking, sneaky slick bastard.

"Sorry, Pip, you are right, it's not my line of work but… I think I might be able to point you in the direction of someone who can help you. This is Lawrence Green's number," and she passed across a business card. "He's a solicitor who handles these types of cases. He has connections and knows the drill. Tell him I sent you. Here's my contact card as well, that way he'll know your legit. Trust him, Pip. He's a good man."

"Thanks, Lori. You're a star. And thanks for the coffee and chat. Sorry, but I've got to dash. Kids to pick up from school. Gymnastics tonight, so it's an early tea," and Phillipa stood ready to leave.

"By the way, Pip, secure what money you can. That's usually one of the first things a cheater protects. His money. Lawrence will no doubt explain all that to you, but it's better if you are prepared with details of the finances if you can before you go see him. Enjoy the gym. Bye."

After she had left, Rob, moved from the table he

had been sitting at to join her.

"Everything okay Gov?" he said.

"You do know you can call me, Lorraine, or Lori, when we're on our own, don't you?"

"Sorry, a force of habit… sweetheart," and he laughed.

"Cheeky." But she too laughed.

Leaving the coffee shop, Phillipa felt a lot better. Even though Lorraine hadn't done very much for her, she had still boosted her confidence and made her believe she could get this matter with Roland resolved. As soon as she could she would contact the solicitor and start the ball rolling. But, for now, she needed to concentrate on the kids and tea.

PHILLIPA

Legal meeting…

Seven days later, Phillipa was shown into the office of Lawrence Green, Solicitor. Shaking hands Mr. Green invited her to sit down and offered her some refreshments which she politely declined.

"Well, it's nice to meet you, Mrs. Fitzpatrick. As you know my name is Lawrence Green, and if we are going to work together I don't mind you calling me by my Christian name. I find it helps my clients to feel more relaxed. You tell me your preference."

Despite her trepidation at meeting Mr. Green, Phillipa found herself smiling at his calm manner. "Thank you, Lawrence it is then. And you can call me Phillipa if you like."

"Good. So now we have that settled, tell me how do you know Chief Inspector Watson, Lorraine?"

A little surprised by the question, Phillipa said, "Oh… err… Lori, Lorraine and I went to the same school. We were in the same class and on the netball team together. We never thought she'd join the police!"

"Okay. She's a good copper and has made a great Chief Inspector. I'll be honest with you, I did have a quick chat with her before agreeing to meet with you and take your case. So, now we have all that out of the way, tell me about your husband... err... Roland is it?"

Nodding her head, Phillipa took a breath and began her tale. She told Lawrence about how they had met, what their plans had been, how they had had to come home to look after his parents, and why she thought her husband was cheating on her. Finally, she said, "I've been finding receipts in the rubbish. For expenses and gifts that seem to have nothing to do with the family. I also managed to log into his personal credit card account and printed the statements off."

Passing the printouts across the desk, Lawrence was a little surprised that she had had the foresight to do this. "Wow, clever girl, Phillipa, well done," as he quickly scanned them.

"Roland is always forgetting his passwords, so he has them written in a small diary which he keeps locked away in the drawer of his desk at home. A few months ago he lost the key and he had to have a locksmith come in and change the lock. When the bill arrived, Roland left a cheque for me to post to them. So, I opened the envelope, found out the locksmith's address, and called into his office to deliver the cheque. Whilst there I asked if he had a duplicate of the key. I made an excuse that Roland was always losing his keys so he had changed his mind about having a second copy. I told the man he wanted me to get a spare which he would lock away in the home safe. I must have been very convincing because he got me one straight away," and Phillipa smiled at her devious behaviour.

She had felt good that day. For a start she had got away with it, paying for the key in cash, and then getting the receipt, which she had destroyed. Roland would never know what she had done.

Lawrence looked at her. "Okay. I see you have marked some items. Can you tell me what they are, please?"

"Sure," and Philippa started to explain what she thought each payment on the card statement had been for. Surprisingly there were many gift items.

"And, none of these gifts were for you, even though they are things like perfume, ear-rings, negligée, underwear, etc.?"

"Hell, no," responded Phillipa, feeling both disgusted and sad. "The last time Roland bought me anything like that was at least five years ago, and that was a flannelette nighty. That's not exactly something you can buy at Victoria's Secrets is it?"

Lawrence smiled in sympathy, thinking for a moment as he looked at the woman sitting in front of him. He had met and dealt with many women in her situation, sometimes plain-looking, sometimes overweight due to birthing children, often tired out from working, looking after children, and running a home. Women whose husbands had gone for a younger model, not realising he was giving up a treasure who had given the best years of her life in serving him. As far as Lawrence was concerned, a lot of men did not deserve the women they had in their lives. Phillipa Fitzpatrick was no different. The difference here was that she was still a fairly attractive woman, even if a little overweight. But to him she had curves, making her someone you would want to cuddle up to on a cold winter night. Any night, if you had any sense.

Pulling himself together, Lawrence realised he had been lost in thoughts he never normally had. Suddenly he became aware that Phillipa was looking at him, a questioning look on her face.

Clearing his throat, he said, "Right! Erm... Right. We need a plan of action. Err... I'm going to suggest we look at putting a private detective on your husband."

"I don't think I can afford one of those? Will he be very expensive?" interrupted Phillipa sounding concerned at the suggestion.

"No, no, err... don't you worry about it. What will happen is, he will spend a certain amount of time following Roland and finding out what he's up to. Then once we have the evidence we can go ahead with the divorce proceedings… you do want to get divorced don't you?"

Surprised, that he had asked, she cocked her head to one side and asked herself, 'Do I want a divorce?'

Finally, she replied, "Yes, Lawrence, I do want a divorce. Roland has taken me for a fool for long enough. It's time he paid for his cheating. Let's go for it. He's worth quite a bit of money so I want my boys to have their share." And for once she sounded positive and adamant in her decision.

Smiling at her, Lawrence said, "That's great, Phillipa. Okay, here is what is going to happen…" and he proceeded to explain the plan he had in mind.

When Phillipa left Lawrence Green's office that day she felt as if she was walking on air. If Lawrence was as good as Lorraine says he was then between them they would show Roland not to mess about with them.

PHILLIPA

The end draws near...

It took three months to get enough 'dirt' on Roland Fitzpatrick, and boy did the PI do his job well. With Roland away on business, Phillipa paid a visit to Lawrence. Giving her an update, she was gob-smacked at the amount of information and evidence the PI had gathered. It even included details of his business, a secret apartment Roland had purchased as a love nest, plus some secret bank accounts he had that she knew nothing about.

"By the time I have finished with Roland, Phillipa, he will regret ever looking at another woman, believe you me."

Phillipa smiled at him. "So, what happens next?"

"Well, I'll apply for a court date. As soon as Roland returns, we'll serve divorce papers on him at his business. In the meantime, I suggest you go home, pack his suitcases for him, and change the locks. Okay?"

"Err... yes, okay."

"Will you need help? Do you know anyone who can stay with you for a few days?"

Thinking about it, Phillipa said, "I think one or

two of the Musketeers might help me."

"Musketeers?" And Lawrence laughed.

Laughing too, she said, "That was the nickname seven of us girls had in school. You know the Musketeers call – all for one, one for all – well that was us. We had a reunion recently, deciding we won't let out friendship slip again. So, if one of us needs help, then at least one or two of the others will be available to help them."

Laughing again, Lawrence said, "Wow, that's great. Okay, Phillipa, I'll keep you posted."

As she left Lawrence's office, Phillipa reflected on what a very nice person he was. He had a lovely smile and a nice laugh. *'Could have done with meeting someone like him, instead of smooth, slick Roland, all those years ago!'* and she laughed at her wicked thoughts.

PHILLIPA

The court rules...

Despite Roland Fitzpatrick's smooth, slick way of speaking, his wife divorcing him was one situation he could not talk himself out of. When all the facts were laid out before the court, Roland found himself well and truly stitched up.

Thanks to Lawrence, Phillipa got the house, a third of the business, half the value of the new apartment, and one very large cash settlement. Roland also had to pay her alimony and support the two boys, including all their school fees, up and until they had finished university.

"Why, have you done this to me, Pip?" he asked her as they left the court.

Looking at him, Phillipa was amazed that he honestly couldn't see the reasoning behind it. Taking a deep breath, she said, "Why, Roland? Well, let's start with you reneging on the deal that we would travel the world. That we wouldn't have children. How about my having to give up my dreams to come home and look after your bloody mother and father. Oh! And let's not forget the fact that you have been screwing anything and everything you could get your hands on for the last… what? Shall we say five years, or maybe it could be ten years. Who the hell knows. But, to be honest, I no longer care. You have been secretive, kept me on a shoestring, spent money on other women, not spent any time with your kids, never been there when they needed their dad. Hell Roland, do you want me to carry on, or have you got the message yet? You have treated me like shit for years. And I have had enough. So, thanks for my children, cause that's about the only good thing that has come out of our relationship. And I can assure you that the men they are going to become won't be down to you, nor will they be like you. Not while I live and breathe. That's it, Roland. Bye. I won't say it's been nice knowing because, to be honest, I'm not sure it ever has been," and upon that note, Phillipa turned and walked away.

* * * * *

Several weeks later, Phillipa was shown into Lawrence Green's office.

"Well, well, well, look at you, Phillipa, very nice and very smart," Lawrence told her.

And she did look smart. But why shouldn't she having been taken under Melinda's wing, being shown how to shop for clothes that would complement her fuller figure. Melinda had also encouraged her to have her hair styled and the colour changed. The difference was remarkable.

Well, Lawrence Green certainly thought so.

"Take a seat. Tell me, how are you doing, although, by the looks of you, you are doing great."

"I am, thank you. I came to say thank you, and to bring you this," and she held out an envelope.

"Err… I thought you'd paid me already?"

"Oh, it's not a cheque. It's an invite to my birthday party. You helped me so much, I wanted to do something nice for you."

Opening the envelope, Lawrence pulled out the invitation and read it.

"It's been many years since I had a birthday party. Roland and the boys always had celebration parties but never me. So, I thought, why not. The eldest boy has gone off to Uni and the youngest is visiting his father for a month during the holidays. So, will you come?"

Looking up, he smiled, "Of course. I would love to come… as long as I get to give you a birthday kiss?" and he looked at her questioningly and hopefully.

Standing, she smiled at him, saying, "Well, let's see what happens, shall we. Oh, by the way, tell me when you were younger and had a party did you ever do sleepovers?"

Laughing, he said, "All the time. Why?"

"No reason. I was thinking that perhaps if you wanted, but only if you wanted, you might like to do a sleepover that night?"

Standing, Lawrence moved around the desk to stand in front of her. Looking deep into her eyes, he said, "Are you sure your dad won't mind?"

Giggling she replied, "Oh, no, he won't mind. He's away on holiday and I'll be **ALL** alone in the house."

Leaning forward, Lawrence gently touched his lips to hers, then said, "Well, we can't have that, can we? I think I'll just have to come and keep you company, won't I."

"I'll err... see you next Saturday then, Lawrence," and Phillipa moved towards the door.

As she left he said, "You certainly will, Pip, you certainly will."

COLEEN

Unusual proposition…

Leaving Melinda's home, Coleen had been left with a lot to think about. For a start, Melinda's confession about her lifestyle and how she had come into her wealth, had floored her. The reminder about those last few weeks of school, and prior, when poor Mel had been suffering at the hands of her older brother, not in a nice way, had upset her. It was worse than she remembered. At least her brother was not like that. He had always respected her boundaries, but since the accident he had become overprotective, behaving more like a father than her da' did.

While she loved her home, life was becoming claustrophobic. And she knew that should she ever get the chance to meet someone, they and her, would get the third, fourth and fifth degree of interrogation before being allowed in the house. It seemed to her that her life was destined to be that of a nun without joining the convent. What was she to do?

A few days later, Melinda, called to see her. "So, are you going home?" she asked.

Smiling, Coleen sat and thought for a moment before speaking. "I've told them I am staying a couple more weeks. Err… I'm glad you've called as I wanted to talk to you about what we discussed the other day. You know…"

"Are you sure?" Coleen nodded her head, yes. "Okay, what do you want to know?"

"Well, tell me what I would have to do?"

Sitting down in the chair, Melinda took a folder from her bag. She had had a feeling that Coleen might have some questions, so had come prepared.

"Let's start with what is possible. Okay. There are different roles you could take. Let's begin with being a hostess. This is where you sit at the table with a customer and talk nicely to him. You would have to wear a sexy outfit. Ply him with a drink, as that is how we make a lot of our income. Maybe let him kiss and occasionally fondle you. And that's it. Sounds a little grubby but you would only be seated with those we know are kind to our hostesses. We don't put up with rough behaviour so you would in most cases be treated respectfully. These are the type of men who want to feel they are looking after you because you are an invalid. Sounds a bit sick but these guys genuinely care. They have probably looked after their mothers or wives and have a need to go on being carers."

"Really. Are there people like that? Wow. What a strange world you live in, Mel."

Laughing, Melinda said, "Oh! Col, it can get a

lot weirder. The second stage of carer wants to care for you. This is where you become the invalid for him to care. It means him undressing you and possibly washing you all over. Then he will re-dress you. He will want to touch you where he shouldn't but he won't, he will only look. So, he may keep your legs open longer, and wash you there longer than he should when using a washcloth but, he won't physically touch you."

Coleen swallowed, beginning to wonder if she was right in her head to even think of doing any of this. But, she realised that if she wanted her independence then maybe needs must. "Okay," she said. "What's next."

Melinda looked at her, surprised Coleen hadn't thrown up yet. Perhaps at the next stage, she just might.

"Okay, the next stage is those men who want to be a carer and who want to do all the above, only they also want to touch. This could mean kissing you, playing with your tits, kissing and sucking them, and even playing your pussy. They may also tell you what a naughty girl you are for letting them do that to you. Or, they may want to turn you over and spank you. How hard is down to you? There would be a secure word that means 'stop' that you would call out when you've had enough spanking. There are also those 'carers' who will want to go all the way and have sex with you. To some men who have been carers of their wives, this is the ultimate goal," and Melinda paused to allow the details to sink in.

"Also, there are some men who just want to have sex with an invalid. The fact you wouldn't be able to move means you are in their control. We can wheedle these types out if need be. Usually, these types are wanting to do this as a way to show they love you."

Coleen, needed time to think and digest what Melinda had been told. "Does this happen a lot? I mean women who are invalided going on the game?"

Melinda nodded her head. "Surprisingly, I used to pretend to be invalided. These men often give the best fuck. They are usually gentle, caring and boy can they last. They also tip the best."

"Melinda, do ever err... regret going with so many men? Didn't you feel... I don't know..."

"Do you mean cheap? Hell no. My aunt used to tell me – girl you are the best I've ever had in my home. The men pay through the nose and would fight to get inside your knickers. Was there ever any man I didn't like? Maybe one or two. But, security guards were listening in on what was going on. Partly to stop the girls from cheating, and partly to stop any man from abusing the girls. My aunt paid a lot to make sure her girls were the best of the best. But I was the best ever."

Coleen looked at Melinda amazed at her candour and openness. All these years since school while she had been chasing a bad man, for that is what Danny had been, then sitting in her wheelchair, Melinda had been enjoying her life in her own unique way and making her fortune.

"Look, Col, I've given you lots of information. There's lots more in there. I'll leave this with you. Study the folder, think about it, sleep on it and then let me know. If it's not for you don't worry. Our secret, eh?" And she put her arms around Coleen and gently squeezed her.

After Melinda had left, Coleen sat thinking over what Mel had told her. She had always been a good Irish Catholic girl but, ever since what happened with Danny and the accident she had lost her belief. She knew if she went down the same road as Melinda, her da' and brother would never speak to her again. The question though, was could she do it? Could she lay on a bed and allow a strange man, no men, to touch her in her most private areas without reacting badly. Perhaps she should try it out first?

COLEEN

Time moves on…

Fifteen months later…

"Miss. Coleen."

"Yes," Coleen replied, looking up to see a medium-height man of about forty years of age.

"I understand that I am joining you this evening." His voice was gentle, and he spoke with a northern accent. It sounded not quite Scottish but close to it.

"And you are?" she asked.

"Patrick Jackson. May I sit, please."

Indicating he could, Coleen asked if she should order a bottle of champagne. He didn't object.

After the drink had been delivered and poured, Patrick started to ask her questions. What had brought her to London; how old was she; etc.

Finally, Coleen, asked, "And what would Patrick like from me this evening?"

Looking her up and down he paused before saying, "Whatever I can get. BUT… first I just want to talk to you. Is there anywhere more private we can go?"

Coleen had had this sort of request before.

Deciding she liked what she saw, she told him what was available and what it would cost, including the conversation. He readily agreed, so she led him away towards the private rooms at the back.

Her room was more palatial than many of the others. Melinda had insisted on it being that way. She wanted Coleen to feel at ease and to be able to move around as she wanted. Entering the room, Coleen moved towards the bed and waited. The man stood watching.

After about three minutes, Coleen said, "Are you going to lift me onto the bed or not?"

Coming to his senses, Patrick jumped forward and very carefully lifted her out of the chair, laying her carefully on the bed.

As he began to move away, Coleen said, "Are you not going to join me? It's quite cosy on here," and she patted the bed next to her.

Grinning, Patrick, slid onto the bed next to Coleen, not daring to touch her even though he wanted to.

"I won't break, I promise," she told him.

He lay looking at her for at least five minutes. Then he took her in his arms and started kissing her. Any conversation would come later.

* * * * *

Patrick became a regular. Visiting and booking

Coleen every night for the next two weeks. Although she had allowed men to touch her he was the first man she let go all the way. Losing her virginity to him was the most sensual feeling she had ever experienced.

After he had gone Coleen chose to retire early. The lovemaking with Patrick had finally made her realise that she couldn't go on any longer. She would have to talk to Melinda about her feelings.

As it happened the decision would be taken out of her hands. On the evening of his last visit, Patrick asked Coleen to marry him. Surprised, she told him she would think about it. Besides, she still needed to talk to Melinda to get her opinion.

Meeting with Mel, the next day, she asked, "What should I do, Mel? I have spent every night with him. It must have cost him a fortune. Up to now, I have never allowed any man to have sex with me but I couldn't resist him. Now he says he wants to marry me. I just don't know what to do."

Melinda looked at her friend. She knew that look. The indecision. Hell, hadn't she gone through that the day Simon had asked her to live with him?

"I'll tell you what I'll do. Let me talk to Patrick. Let me find out exactly what his game is. Whether he's genuine or not. If he is, and if you love him, which I think you do, then I suggest you go for it. How's that?"

Thinking over what Melinda had said, it dawned

on Coleen that she did in fact love Patrick, and besides, she now knew she was ready to give up the game. If he could accept what she'd done over the last couple of years, and still wanted to marry her, then she would say yes.

"Okay, Mel. You talk to him. Tell him I am unsure about him accepting me after what I have done. But, if he truly loves me as much as he says he does and is willing to overlook all my past then my answer is… yes."

* * * * *

Two months later, Coleen's brother wheeled his sister down the aisle of their local Roman Catholic church. Although Coleen felt a little hypocritical, she had agreed to a church wedding for her da's sake. Waiting near the altar was the padre and her future husband, Patrick with his best man, Billie. Sat in the front pew was her father. He hadn't been able to walk down with her due to suffering from severe arthritis.

Behind Coleen's chair walked Melinda, Zhora, Fran, Susie, Phillipa, and Loraine (the remaining seven musketeers).

The congregation consisted of an assortment of people – from friends, family, ex-working colleagues, and a few selective up-market past clientele.

The latter two had been put on notice that not one of them was to refer to Coleen's past. As far as anyone was concerned Coleen had been working as an assistant to the Honourable Baroness Melinda Fitzherbert.

Their wedding had been paid for by Melinda and her new husband, a very wealthy Baron from France.

* * * * *

Their wedding day had gone well.

Later, as Patrick and Coleen lay in bed together, she looked at him. "Patrick, are you sure about having married me?" she asked.

Looking down at her, he gently took her in his arms. "Coleen, I have loved you since the first moment I saw you when you were fourteen years old. I am so sorry that you went through so much pain and horror. I have not been the best of people in my youth. But we will put all that behind us and we'll spend the rest of our lives living in perfect happiness."

Surprised by his response, she said. "Fourteen! What do you mean you've loved me since I was fourteen? I didn't know you back then. Did I?"

Smiling, Patrick looked at her, before saying, "You lived with your aunt, down the same street as me. We used to smile at each other when we passed. I had a lot more hair then, it was red and I looked like a tomahawk."

Suddenly, Coleen remembered. Now she knew why Patrick had always seemed so familiar. Then smiling at him, she said, "Oh, my. Pat. My Indian Warrior!" and leaning forward they kissed as the years slipped away and they were young once again.

254

FRAN

Becoming a civvie…

Returning to civvie street hadn't been as hard as Fran had expected it to be, although she still missed the army. The ease of her transition was partly due to her parents' welcome, and the reaction she had received at the reunion. Seeing the Musketeers again and hearing all the stories of their lives so far had intrigued Fran. It had, however, taken a few get-togethers before she had finally opened up about her time in the military.

"What, you were wounded," said a shocked Susie.

Fran nodded, "Yes, but it wasn't that bad. Three of my guys got it worse than I did. At least no one had died."

Susie was still amazed and shocked by Fran's revelation. "You are so brave, Fran. I could never have done what you did. So, what you gonna do now?"

Fran thought for a moment. "Not sure. Take it easy for a while. Going to take mom and dad on a holiday to Cornwall to see the relatives. Dad can't drive long distances anymore, so I might as well do it before I start working."

"That's very good of you," said Zhora. "Are they nice? Your family?"

Laughing, Fran said, "To be honest, I don't know. I haven't seen them in twenty years. Been away so long, I've lost touch. Probably wouldn't even recognise them if I met them on the street."

Looking at Zhora, she went on, "I have to say I'm surprised you're married to an English guy. Thought you were up for an arranged married?"

Zhora hesitated before responding. It still hurt to talk about what her brother Rashid had done. "I was, but it all fell through after my oldest brother was arrested. He set a bomb off," and she hung her head in shame.

Leaning forward, Fran, took hold of her hand. "It wasn't your fault, Zhora."

"I know but you were in the army protecting us and he went and did something so horrible. I'll never forgive him."

"We can't take the blame for what other people do. Even those who are related to us. Now, tell me about Ray?" Looking into Fran's eyes, Zhora realised that she truly was a good friend. One of the Musketeers, just as she was and always would be.

I hope Rashid rots in hell,' she thought. 'And my Mother as well!'

The meeting with Zhora had brought home to Fran why she had joined the forces. And how much she was going to miss the regimental format that had been her life. She also knew she had to get a job, but the question was, what could she do? For the moment she wouldn't think about it but concentrate on having a good holiday with her parents. They deserved the trip to Cornwall to visit Dad's sister and family, even if it wasn't her scene, she would make the best of it and ensure her parents enjoyed themselves.

FRAN

The way forward...

Three weeks later after an extended stay in Cornwall, Fran and her parents returned to the peace and quiet of their home. Fran especially was glad to be back. Although used to the noise and turmoil of the army barracks, her aunt's house had been overcrowded practically every day they had been there. It had got so bad that Fran had been up early most mornings, and was out and about, jogging along the local beach, returning as late as she could for breakfast. She always managed to get back in time before her aunt had cleared the table.

After a good night's rest, Fran was once again up early. This time she was off to town to visit the local job centre. Surely there had to be a job she was suitable for. But what that was, she had no idea.

Opening the door to the job centre, Fran looked at the vacancies listed on the wall. "Good-morning, can I help you?"

Turning to see who had spoken, Fran was met by a lady of similar age to herself. "I'm ex-forces, and I'm looking for a job. Trying to see what's available."

Smiling the lady said, "Oh! Do I know you? Have we met before?"

Fran looked closely at the woman, trying to recall if she knew who she was. She wrinkled her eyes up as she flitted through her memory. "Were you in the forces?"

"Yes, I was. I err… I was made to resign." And at that point, it dawned on Fran who she was.

"Mary? Mary Jenkins. As I live and breathe it is you. How are you doing? That was a bum deal you got."

Laughing, Mary nodded her head in agreement. "Sure was, but they couldn't have a lesbian in that man's army could they?"

Fran looked at the young woman. "Things changed a lot after you were pushed out. You caused quite a stir. Made the brass sit up and reassess the role of women in the forces," and Fran held out her hand to shake Marys.

Mary reciprocated. "Thanks. They didn't drum you out, did they?"

Laughing, Fran said, "No. My time was up. Done twenty. Now I need a job."

"Well, you come on over here with me. I know I can help you. There probably won't be anything suitable for you pinned up there," and she pointed at the board before leading the way to a desk at the rear of the centre. "Sit down, Fran, and tell me all about yourself?"

Sitting down, Fran explained how she'd been in the services twenty years. That she had risen to the rank of Captain, a position she had held for ten years and from which she had retired. Then she went on to talk about her active duty; about being wounded, but this, fortunately, hadn't affected her ability to work. After finishing, Fran explained that they had offered her a promotion but it came with a desk job. However, that wasn't really what she had joined the military for. As such, she didn't want a job that was all desk work.

Having finished talking, Mary, looked up and smiled. "Congratulations, and well done. Well, I think we can find something suitable for you. Let me just look at the computer and see what is available."

After searching through the centre's records, Mary said, "I can offer a number of suggestions. From Police, to the prison service, to private security. All will have some form of paperwork involved but won't keep you sitting at a desk all day. What do think?"

"Mmm… possible I suppose. I suppose it will depend on what the position is. Private security, will that involve travelling?"

Mary looked at the job details. "Yes, the job is for a Saudi Prince. Not really you, I suppose."

Fran shook her head.

"Hang on a minute, let me look again," and she returned to the computer. "Ahh… what would you think about being a Customs Officer at the airport?"

At the first mention of Border Force/Customs officer, Fran had been in two minds about the job, but now she wondered what that would entail. "What exactly is the job and where?"

Mary relooked at the details, saying, "Okay, it's at the airport. They are looking for someone who can handle people, can do undercover work. Hey, Fran, this would suit you down to the ground. What do you think? Shall I give them a call?"

Fran thought for a moment, nodded her head, and said, "Yes, why not. Let's give it a go."

FRAN

A new job…

"Morning, Fran," said Senior Officer Jones.

"Morning, Ewen. What's on the agenda today?"

"We've got intel that there's a gang of mules coming through Heathrow on the eleven o'clock flight from Thailand. We're expecting about five or six. Can you go plain clothes and see if you can suss them out, please?"

Smiling, Fran said, "Sure. Any dogs?"

"Yea, you'll have Johnny and Barb with their dogs backing you. It's going to be busy, so good luck," and Jones left her to change back into her civvies.

Doing this kind of work was becoming a regular thing for the Border Force. Sometimes Fran wondered whether it was worth all the effort, but, if they didn't stop it somehow the country would be flooded with drugs and they would lose the fight.

Having changed, Fran made her way down to the arrival's custom department. She carried lightweight hand baggage, something she could drop if she was needed in an emergency. Her job was to saunter up and down the luggage consoles as if waiting for her case, but in reality, she was looking for someone suspicious.

Fran had been carrying out this work for a couple of years now and she fully enjoyed her job. Although there was some paperwork, there was still a smattering of the regimental feeling that she had had in the army. It suited her to a tee.

Since meeting Mary at the job centre they had kindled their friendship from the earlier days when they were first starting in the military. Unfortunately, Mary was very much a lesbian, being quite open about it. While Fran was more unsure as to where her sexual feelings lay. She had experimented after leaving school with a couple of girls but having joined the army she had curbed the urges as she knew it was frowned upon.

Meeting Mary had somehow resurrected those feelings. And over the last eighteen months, with their friendship growing, Fran was starting to feel some affection for her new friend. A few months ago, Mary had intimated that those feelings were returned and they had spent the night in bed enjoying exploring each other's bodies. Within a week they were officially an item.

With Fran's job now being secure, she had decided to ask Mary to marry her. These days same-sex marriage was legal so there was no reason why she shouldn't. No reason that is, except for her parent's reaction. She wasn't sure what they would say about the fact that their ex-forces daughter was gay?

Suddenly her earpiece buzzed. "Operation Siam is a go. Acknowledge."

Raising her hand to her nose, as if to scratch it, Fran lowered her head and quietly spoke into the mic attached to her jacket lapel. "Fran here, it's 'a go'."

FRAN

"Fran, darling," said her mother, pleasantly surprised by the sudden visit of her only child. "What a lovely surprise. Come in? Is something wrong?"

Laughing, Fran kissed her mother on her cheek, saying, "No, mother, nothing is wrong. I had the day off so I thought I would visit you. Is it a crime to want to see one's parents?"

Grabbing her daughter in a big hug, Mrs. Watson laughed, saying, "Oh! Don't be silly. Come on, your father is in the garden," and she led Fran through the house to the rear garden.

Having shared all her news, Fran sat waiting for the coffee her mother had insisted on making her. Silence reigned in the garden. Her father, ever the perceptive man he was, coughed and finally said, "Okay, what's the real reason you're here, in the middle of the week?"

Laughing, Fran looked at her father. Despite his age, he was still a good-looking man. "Ok, I never could get anything past you or keep anything from you, could I?" He shook his head but did not speak, waiting for her to respond.

Taking a couple of breaths, Fran finally spit it out. "I'm thinking of getting married, Dad."

This had been the last thing he had expected to hear from his daughter. Trying not to show his surprise he gently asked, "And do we know the person you are to marry, Frannie?"

"Err… Yes. But I'm not sure how happy you will be about this."

"Why, is she weird or foreign?"

About to answer, Fran stopped as she realised what her father had just said. "You know?" she asked him.

"That you are gay? Yes, of course."

"Mom, as well?"

"Of course, I do, dear," said her mother, coming back into the garden carrying the mug of coffee. "So, tell us all about her? What's her name? And when do we get to meet her?"

Fran could have cried. There she was worried about her parent's reaction yet they knew all along. "How did you know," she asked.

Standing, her father went to hug her, before returning to his seat. As he did he said, "My darling, you are our daughter. We are not blind, nor stupid. And, it doesn't matter who you marry as long as that person makes you as happy as your mother and I have been. We love you."

There were tears all round that afternoon. And also later when Fran told Mary what her parents' reaction had been to the news. Both ladies were happy, arranging to visit Fran's parents the following weekend to discuss their wedding plans.

Later that night, as she lay in bed with Mary asleep in her arms, Fran had never felt as happy or as contented as she did at that moment. Life was good for her. She had left the job she loved, only to find a new job and a new love. Things couldn't have been any better, especially as her parents were once again backing her all the way.

ZHORA

Payback is a Bitch…

Zhora was woken by loud screaming.

It was her mother – again – having a go at Parveen her sister-in-law. Climbing out of the spare bed, she went to discover what had gone wrong. Whatever it was, from her mother's point of view it would be all her daughter-in-law's fault. As far as Zhora was concerned, it would be her mother's! The ungrateful, selfish bitch that she was. Shaking her head to clear the sleep from her mind she regretted having agreed to stay and help care for her mother while her younger brother, Parveen's husband, was away visiting their elder brother Rashid, who had been moved to a more secure prison. As far as Zhora was concerned they could lock Rashid up and throw away the key.

As Zhora walked into the room she heard. "You lazy, good for nothing, pig." It was her mother yelling loudly, as she lashed out at poor Parveen.

"Mother, stop that. How dare you?" yelled Zhora, seeing Parveen curled up on the floor trying to protect herself.

Her mother raised the leather belt she was holding and lashed out again at the quivering young woman.

Dashing across to the bed, Zhora grabbed the belt and yanked it from her mother's grip. "You bitch. You mean, ungrateful, bitch."

Her mother looked at her shocked. Then as if gathering her second steam she launched into a tirade of foul language, aimed at Zhora, at Zhora's husband Ray, and finally at Paveen. The spiteful, vicious look on her face both surprised and shocked Zhora. Before she could help herself, Zhora crossed the room back to the bed and slapped her mother hard across the face.

"Don't... you... ever... dare... speak... about my husband like that again or, so help me, I will kill you, you bitch." This time the venom with which Zhora had spoken attracted her mother's attention.

About to open her mouth to speak, Zhora jumped in, saying, "Don't. Don't utter one single word, because if you do, as Allah is my witness I will take this belt and I will beat the living daylights out of you. Now lay down and be quiet while I see to the damage you have done to Parveen," then turning her back she helped her sister-in-law up from the floor and guided her from the bedroom.

An hour later once Parveen had calmed down, Zhora having seen to the wounds on her face inflicted by the belt her mother had wielded, Zhora put the kettle on and made some tea. Sitting down she spoke to her sister-in-law.

"How long has she been like this?"

Parveen, obviously afraid to answer for fear of retribution from her husband, hung her head and shrugged her shoulders.

Zhora looked at her. "Parveen, I need to know how many times has she hit you? And if you are afraid of what Saleem will say, forget it, I will sort that little turd out when he gets home. So, how many times has she hit you?"

For a moment, Parveen didn't move, then slowly she undid her kameez bearing her upper body. Turning Parveen displayed her back, arms and stomach.

What Zhora saw shocked and sickened her. Looking at her gentle, timid sister-in-law, she asked, "Who did this? My mother? Saleem? Who? And why?"

Shaking with fright and embarrassment, Parveen finally whispered, "Both of them. They take turns in beating me," and she paused before suddenly saying quickly, "It is because I am a slow learner and do not get the jobs done properly or quick enough. The house is always dirty. I do not clean it well enough. And the food is never cooked as Saas requires. It is my fault."

Standing up, Zhora felt she was about to

explode. Her instinct was to go into her mother's room and beat the hell out of her. She needed to think. Clear her head. She would talk to Ray. He would know what to do.

"Parveen put your kameez back on, then go and lie down."

"But what about Saas? She will expect me to serve her some food and drink. And to wash her."

"You do as I say. I will see to my mother. For now, I want you to rest," and she smiled.

Parveen had left the room, leaving Zhora to sit, deciding what to do. Finally, she had a plan. First thing was to give her mother something to eat and drink. Making her a cup of tea and some porridge she took the food into her mother's bedroom.

"About time," her mother grumbled. "Where is that lazy, no good pi… girl?"

Zhora looked at her mother. Then taking a breath she said, "Parveen has gone to lie down."

Her mother opened her mouth to speak but before any words came out, Zhora said, "Shut it. If you so much as say one word against Parveen I will take this food and give it to the dogs on the street and you will go without. There are two good for nothing, lazy, pigs in this house and that is Saleem and you. Now, I am going to leave the food here on the table. If you want it, you can get out of bed and eat. If you can't be bothered to move your fat behind then you will starve because I am not going to wait on you any longer," and with that she placed the tray she was carrying on the table then turning she left the room, slamming the door behind her.

Calming herself down, Zhora picked up her phone and rang Ray. Fortunately, her husband was free to talk to her. The minute he came on the phone he knew she was upset. What's happened, my darling?"

Taking a breath so she could control her emotions she calmly told him what had happened and what she had discovered. Ray was as shocked as Zhora had been. He knew his estranged mother-in-law was an unpleasant woman but beating a defenceless timid creature like Paveen was a step too far.

"I'm coming over. Now," he told her, broking no arguments. He hadn't wanted her to stay for the couple of nights while Saleem was away; only readily agreeing when Zhora had reassured him everything would be fine. But this was too much. If Saleem was beating his wife then upon returning and having found she'd interfered in his family lifestyle he could well turn on his sister. And if there was one thing Ray would not stand, not just as a Lawyer, but as a husband and a man it was wife being beaten.

Ending the call he had his secretary cancel the rest of the days' appointments and within fifteen minutes was driving out of the city on his way to his mother-in-law's residence. All the time he was doing his best to retain some control over his anger.

ZHORA

A brother pays...

Saleem did not arrive home until the following day and was surprised to find the house in darkness. Entering through the front door, he called out, "Ammi... I'm back." There was no answer.

Next, he called for his wife, "Paveen, where are you? Come here now!" Still no response. Now he was starting to wonder what had happened? Where was his wife, but more importantly, where was his mother?

Walking into the living room, Saleem finally noted the envelope with his name on it, sitting on the fireplace. Picking it up he tore it open, taking out the letter from inside, he began to read. Saleem was stunned.

"What!" he shouted.

The contents of the letter read as follows:

Saleem,
This is to inform you that Paveen has left you. She has been placed in a home for abused women. The Police have already been notified and statements have been taken regarding the abuse that both you and our mother have committed against her. Do not try and

find out where she is, or go anywhere near her. If you do, the people in charge of the home are under strict instructions from the police to ring them and you will be arrested.

As regards our mother she too is being charged with assault. In the meantime, she has been placed in a mental institution for the criminally insane. Her behaviour towards Paveen has been both cruel and sadistic, and I will no longer allow her, or you to continue abusing an innocent girl like Paveen for your sadistic tastes.

Do not think of contacting me, as I have no wish to speak to you. I have given my statement to the police and Ray has organised a restraining order. A copy of it is on the kitchen table. If you attempt to come anywhere near me, or our property, believe me, I will call the police and have you thrown in prison.

Enjoy the house while you can, you have three days in which to pack only your belongings and leave. After that, I will take action to have you removed from the property. Don't take anything that doesn't belong to you as I will report you to the police for theft.

Remember, I do have a full record and photographs of the contents.

You see Saleem, there has been one thing you have always forgotten about me, and that is, that when our brother needed money for his defence he came to *me for the cash. No one else would help him. So, yes, I gave it to him, but only on the condition that he signed the house over to me. At the time I did it to keep a roof over our mother's head. Well, she won't need it any longer. And you are no longer welcome in it either. As for Parveen, she is going to need money to start her new life so I shall be selling the house to help her get a divorce and to go as far away from you as she can.*

You are as much a sadistic sick bastard as Rashid and our mother. Our father must be turning his grave.

Zhora

ZHORA

Happy news...

After the reunion, Zhora, with Ray's encouragement had reforged her friendship with the other Musketeer girls. He had seen her face lighten when she talked about any of them and knew she was happier than she had been for some time.

Time had moved on. Two years had passed since Zhora had sorted the problem of her mother and brother out. Her brother Saleem had had enough sense to accept that he was up against it, especially as Ray was a top-notch lawyer. Besides his sister was a hard nut and he knew she wouldn't give him an inch.

In time, Zhora's mother lost her mind. After having a had severe heart attack she had passed away. Zhora hadn't visited her at the sanitorium where, after being removed from the house, she had been locked away for her own safety. However, she and Ray did pay for the funeral.

Although Saleem had attended the service, he had kept his distance, being too afraid to approach, even though he had wanted to speak to them. But what could he say? 'That he was sorry? Yet was he? When had it all gone wrong? Hell, this was all Rashid's fault.

No. It was his mother's fault – no wonder Zhora hated them all.' Leaving the mosque he had walked away, knowing he would never speak to his sister again.

As for Zhora's oldest brother, Rashid, he had taken his own life. Or maybe he had been helped along the way. His arrogant attitude whilst in prison had probably proved to be his undoing. From what Ray could find out, Rashid had crossed the wrong man and was later found hanging in his cell one morning. Zhora did not attend his burial nor did she shed a tear at his loss.

"Gone and forgotten," she told her husband.

He wondered if she was as hard as she pretended to be, knowing that maybe one day she would cry for her family. And, when she did, he would be there to hold her in his arms to show her how much he loved her.

* * * * *

About two weeks later, Ray got an urgent message from Zhora. "I need you to come home, now, please."

Ray was starting to panic, asking her, "What's Wrong, sweetheart? Tell me?"

"No. Come home," and she hung up the phone.

As he drove through the busy city streets Ray worried over what had happened to his wife. *'Had Saleem suddenly shown up on their doorstep? If he had he would kill him especially if he had hurt her.'*

He began trying to work out what was so urgent that he had to leave his office. *'She would have phoned the police. Been more panicky! Hell, he hated it when she did things like this to him.'*

Twenty minutes later, having only just kept within the speed limits, Ray pulled his Mercedes car into the driveway of their home. Jumping out of the car, he grabbed his briefcase, quickly locked the car, and dashed inside.

"Honey, Zho, where are you? What's wrong? What's happened," he shouted as he raced along the hallway into the lounge.

Stopping in the doorway, he found his wife sitting on the sofa. There was a big grin across her face and tears were running down her cheeks.

Rushing across the room he took her in his arms, saying, "Whatever it is, I'll sort it. I don't care what it is. Tell me?"

Laughing, Zhora looked up into the eyes of the man she loved, itching to spring her surprise on him. Patting the seat on the settee next to her, he sat down, finally calming down as he discovered she was safe.

"Okay," he said. "Tell me what was so urgent that I had to drive home without any due care for the speed limits? And me, a court lawyer."

Reaching behind her, Zhora pulled out a small black and white photograph. Or at least it looked like a photograph. That is until you looked closer.

Turning it around so Ray could see the image, his eyes opened wide. He looked at Zhora, then back at the photo, before looking back at his wife. She was smiling from ear to ear.

"Is that… what… I think… it is?"

Nodding her head, Zhora said, "Yes. We're going to have a baby."

All at once, the smile faded from her face, as suddenly she thought that maybe Ray didn't want children. After all, they had never talked about it.

"Are you cross about it?"

As a huge smile crossed her husband's face, he said, "Cross! Hell, no. I think it's bloody marvellous. I'm going to be a dad. Wow! Let me look again?"

Later, as they sat cuddling on the sofa, Zhora asked, "You really are pleased about it, aren't you, Ray."

Moving to look deep into her eyes, Ray said, "My darling, this is the best news I've ever had. Are you happy about becoming a mom? After… you know, with you know who…?"

"You mean, my mother."

Looking sheepishly at her, Ray nodded his head.

"My mother was evil when there was no need to

be. I will not be like her. Our child, son, or daughter will be brought up with lots of love. Allah has ordained it because its parents both love and respect each other. As long as I have you by my side, my darling husband, I am happy."

* * * * *

Seven months later, Zhora and Ray welcomed not one, but two children into the world – Twins. The girl they named Amira (meaning princess) Charlotte (after Zhora's mother-in-law) and the boy, Aryan (meaning noble and high-born) Raymond (after his father).

They were baptised into the Christian church, even though Ray had agreed they could be accepted into the Muslim religion. Zhora had declined his suggestion, saying she was perfectly happy for them to follow their fathers faith. Besides, they could always choose to change once they grew up.

Zhora's in-laws had always been welcoming of her, more so than her family had ever been of Ray. Although it was never spoken about she knew this decision would please them. And, as a good wife and daughter-in-law, she wished to honour them by choosing their religion.

Life for Zhora would be far more settled as her children, and her beloved husband was now the centre of her world.

LORRAINE

A new romance…

As the evening of the reunion drew to a close, Smithy, sitting with his arm resting around Lorraine's shoulders, whispered in her ear, "You ready for the off, Lori?"

Turning to look at him, she smiled, "Err, well I've booked a room in the B & B down the street. A double room… if you're interested?"

Looking at her, he smiled. "It took you long enough to ask," he said. "Come on then let's go. The night is still young and I have a lot to show you."

Laughing she, said, "Are you bragging or what?"

Joining in the laughter he replied, "That's for you to say… Gov."

Saying good night to the other Musketeers, Lorraine and Smithy left the room. After they had gone, Susie said, "Do you reckon they have a thing going?"

Ray said, "If they didn't have before, I bet after tonight they will," and he laughed, saying "ouch," as Zhora his wife playfully slapped him.

* * * * *

That night with Rob Smith was a turning point

for Lorraine. For the first time in a long time, she took a serious look at her life. But in particular, she assessed the type of men she had been involved with in the past. She started with her past relationship with Mark.

Like Mark, Rob was younger than her. It made her wonder if she was perhaps trying to capture her lost youth by falling for another toyboy. Not that Rob could be classed as a one considering he was only just over nine years younger than her. Still, having been hurt and treated badly by Mark, Lorraine was wary of falling into the same trap.

As it turned out she wasn't the only one who was having some thoughts about forming a relationship. If Rob was honest he had had the hots for Lori since she had first become his Governor. Maybe he liked being bossed around by older women. The thought made him chuckle to himself. The other worry for him was that she was his boss and the force might not approve of a subordinate dating a senior officer. If they did start dating then they would have to be careful and keep it under the radar.

LORRAINE

Going forwards…

Twelve months had passed since the first time Rob and Lorraine had slept together. It was a night she had not forgotten. Whilst he had certainly been bragging, being true to his word, he had still known how to satisfy her. In fact, sex with Rob was far, far better than it had ever been with Mark.

A couple of months later Rob had moved into her house.

Entering work that morning she received a message that the Police Commissioner wished to speak to her. Ringing his office she had arranged to go see him that afternoon. All morning her mind had been working overtime, wondering if someone had seen her and Rob out together and had reported them. Rob was on a course that day, having left home early, so she couldn't contact him to forewarn him.

Arriving at the Commissioner's office, Lorraine ran her hands down the skirt of her uniform. She was nervous, having no clue about the summons. Sitting waiting, her mouth felt dry and she wished she had a bottle of water to hand.

"Chief Inspector Watson? Come this way please."

Following the secretary through the door into the office she discovered the Commissioner and the Mayor plus a couple of people sat at a table, waiting for her.

"Take a seat, Chief Inspector," said the Commissioner, pointing to a chair at the end of the table. "Err... Ladies and Gentlemen, please introduce yourselves." Each person sat at the table spoke their name and their position and department in turn.

"Now, Chief Inspector Watson, or can I call you Lorraine?"

Lori acquiesced to his request with a nod of her head, and a small, "Of course."

"Good. Now, Lorraine, we have called you here to have a discussion with you, which by the way is off-record at the moment, about a new incentive the Mayor is wanting to introduce."

Lorraine breathed a quiet sigh of relief. They hadn't wanted to discuss her relationship with Rob at all. Relieved she sat up and listened intently as the Commissioner continued explaining. By the end of his speech, it turned out that the Mayor wanted to instigate a new protocol about encouraging more females to become police officers. Particularly within the minority sections of the community. As a Chief Inspector, and a woman, the panel wanted her opinion, her professional and personal input, and whether or not she could give them guidance as to how they could set this new incentive up.

Two hours later, Lorraine, having advised the panel as much as she could, returned to her office, feeling relieved. The only problem was she couldn't tell Rob what had happened just yet.

LORRAINE

Promotion for who?...

Two months later, Lorraine finally received notice
about the new incentive. Having given lots of thought
to the situation, she concluded that perhaps it was the
Commissioners' way of getting rid of her. After all, she
had been on the force for some years now.

Attending the Commissioner's office she was
informed that they would like her to spearhead the new
campaign – Operation Ladybird. The aim was to
encourage young women of all nationalities born in the
UK to consider joining the police force.

"To be honest, Commissioner, I would prefer it
if you found someone else. I think the incentive is an
amazing thing but I enjoy the job I currently do. Can
you not find someone else to take on the role, please?"

The Commissioner looked at her for a moment,
then he said, "Lorraine, you are and always have been
a good officer. And while I understand your desire to
continue working in the position you are in, it's time
for a change. Time to move on and let someone else
step up to the mark. You have so much experience, I
know that. And this incentive is only for twelve
months.

After that, I want to promote you further up the

ladder. Give you more control, perhaps move you to a different department. In the meantime, I also want to let the officers beneath you have their chance. What about this young man, Robert Smith. Do you think he'd make a good Chief? Or maybe Martin Cross, what about him?"

Lorraine swallowed. *'Hell,'* she thought. *'I'm being outed by my boyfriend.'*

"Obviously if you think neither of them isn't good enough, you just say the word."

"Err… no, Sir. Both are good officers and well capable of taking over the job. It's a question of which one to choose. In order of seniority, it would have to be Smith."

"But, something is bothering you, Lorraine. What is it?"

Lorraine took a moment to gather her thoughts. Finally, she said, "Are you trying to get rid of me, Sir?"

The Commissioner looked shocked at her comments. Then smiling, he said, "No, Lorraine, I am not. I wasn't going to say this yet, but between you and I, you are in line for the Chief Super's job?"

"What! Are you serious, Sir?"

Smiling at her, the Commissioner said, "Yes, Lorraine, I am. O' Malley is due to retire next year and they want a woman in the job. You are being highly recommended. Would you take it if offered the post?"

"Phew. Hell, yes, Sir, I would. It's the dream job for someone like me," and she grinned at him.

Grinning back, he said, "As I said, it's hush-hush at the moment. Just so you know, O' Malley agrees with the choice. This is why we are keeping his retirement quiet. Take this new incentive job. Set it up, get the right crew on board and run it for nine months. Then get ready to take the new job. Our secret, okay?" and he rose to shake her hand. "Well done, and congratulations, Lorraine."

"Thank you, Sir. I'm honoured." Standing she shook his hand and then turning she started to leave his office.

"By the way, Lorraine. The move will give you the chance to marry that young man of yours, won't it?"

A surprised look came across her face. "Young man, Sir? Mark and I broke up some time ago."

Looking at Lorraine for a moment, finally, the Commissioner, tapped the side of his nose. "Who said anything about Mark. I meant the new young man. What's his name – Rob, isn't it? Rob Smith? He'll make a good Chief Inspector as well as a great husband. Our secret, Lorraine, our secret," and he laughed lightly at the shocked expression on her face.

"Err… you know?" she whispered.

"Chief Inspector Watson, there isn't anything I don't know about my officers. That's how I've managed to stay in this job for so long. You remember that. Good luck."

"I will. And thank you, Sir," and she quickly left the office.

As Lorraine walked down the corridor and out of the building, she thought, *'Well, I never. The sneaky old devil,'* and she chuckled. What a surprise Rob was going to have when she told him.

SUSIE

Laughter is the best cure...

The reunion had proven to be a good thing for Susie. After all, she had gone through with the death of her husband Ted, Susie needed help to cope. Yes, she had her only child, Debbie, but the Musketeers were her age and proved to be just the right support she needed. Thus allowing her daughter to carry on leading her own life. Finding your husband, the man you had loved since you were sixteen years old, had not only deserted you but had also betrayed you after all the years you had devoted to him had a devastating impact on her confidence and belief in the human race, but especially men.

The Musketeers had quickly been drawn back together, almost as though the years had never passed. At the reunion, they had chatted and laughed as if they were once again those fifteen/sixteen-year-olds; celebrating their ups and downs together. That evening they had sat, each recalling their memories about their school days. By the end of the evening, Susie had relaxed and had begun to enjoy herself.

A few days later, Coleen, Melinda, and Susie had met at a local restaurant to chat. Melinda was quite open about what had happened to her. How her brother and his friend had raped her. About her going on the game with her aunt and finally her running the best brothel in London. Coleen had also talked about the death of her aunt in the ambush, her mother dying, and how she had ended up in a wheelchair. Susie was amazed at their frankness and honesty.

As they chatted, Melinda asked, "So, how did you get it together with Teddy Smith, Suz?"

"Do you remember him?" Susie asked.

Melinda and Coleen laughed together. "I think we all remember, Ted. He was hot." And all three laughed.

Once they were calmer Susie said, "It just happened," and she went on to tell them how they started seeing each other, then her getting pregnant, meaning they had to get married. "My mother was not pleased about that one," said Susie. "Mind you, Dad was great and my brother, Justin, was also supportive. Anyway, we did okay I suppose. Debs was the result."

"When did he die?" asked Coleen.

"Twelve weeks ago. He left me. Out of the blue."

Melinda looked sad for her. "Another woman, Suz?"

Susie made a sort of sharp, short laugh, "I wish. That's something I could have lived with. No. He left me for another man."

"What!" said Melinda and Coleen together, shock written across their faces. Neither could believe that they were talking about the same Teddy Smith. At school, he had been every girls, 'wished for boyfriend.' Certainly never showing any gay tendencies.

"The worst thing for him was that he was that eager to get to his boyfriend, he crashed the car and killed himself. Arsehole!!" continued Susie.

There was silence for a few minutes then all at once, all three girls cracked up in fits of laughter, causing everyone in the restaurant to turn their way to see what the commotion was all about.

Finally settling down, Susie said, "Thanks, girls. That's the first good laugh I've had for weeks. Wow, I feel so much better," and they all started laughing again.

SUSIE

Life goes on…

A few weeks later, Zhora rang Susie to ask her if she would like to go out for dinner. There were to be seven of them, and they had a friend who would be the odd one out, so Zhora wondered if she would like to make the party up to eight and keep her friend company. No strings, just dinner, and a drink.

Susie had been reluctant. After all, she had never been out with anyone else since starting to date Ted. The idea was both frightening and exciting. Zhora could sense her reluctance, so told her not to worry, that James was a nice guy and a gentleman. He was one of Ray's buddies, and wouldn't put any pressure on her. Finally, convinced, Susie took the bull by the horns and agreed to go.

* * * * *

On the Saturday following, Susie left the house, taking a taxi to The Maharaja Club, Indian Restaurant, on the high street. Strangely, Ted had never fancied Indian food but she had, so when he was working away she would order a take-away from their local curry house.

This evening Susie was dressed in a new blue-green trouser suit that brought out the colour of her eyes. She had a delightful cream blouse underneath and wore a darker blue jacket over the top. She had even gone and had her hair cut and styled. For the first time in a long time, Susie felt alive.

However, as she approached the restaurant the nerves began to kick in. Her steps slowed and the closer she got to the door the more unsure she became of entering the place. About to turn and run, a voice said, "Are you, Susie?"

Stopping, Susie turned and looked straight into the most gorgeous pair of blue eyes she had ever seen on anyone, let alone a man. He was looking at her, with a smile and a questioning look.

"Err… yes. I'm Susie. And you are…"

"James. James Haydon. Pleased to meet you. Zhora described you exactly. She said you might be a bit nervous entering a strange place alone, so I said I would come outside and look for you. Are you okay?"

"Yes… Yes. Hello, James, it's nice to meet you. I'm Suz… oh! You know who I am don't you," and they both laughed. Susie found his laugh warm.

He had spoken gently to her. "Well, shall we go in? Or do you want to run away somewhere?"

Laughing she said, "What! And miss the evening. Lead the way, James."

Gently taking her arm, he smiled and said,

"Good. I've heard nothing about you, other than you are very nice, so let's get to know each other a bit more, shall we?"

The evening went with a swing, with James and Susie soon getting engrossed in conversation. He allowed her to talk about her recent bereavement. And he explained how he had lost his wife nearly eighteen months previous. They discovered they liked the same types of films and music; and they both loved to dance, although Susie hadn't done much of that in recent years as Ted had gone off the idea.

At the end of the meal, James asked if he could walk Susie to the taxi rank, saying I would offer to drive you home, but as this is only the first time we've met I don't want you to feel obligated to invite me in for a nightcap if I do," and he laughed lightly.

Smiling at him, she said, "Thank you. That's very considerate of you."

"What would you say to us meeting up for a coffee one lunchtime. Or maybe you'd consider having dinner with me?" he tentatively asked.

She liked James. And even though it had only been a few weeks since Ted's death she knew their marriage had been dead long, long before that.

"Why don't we start with lunch one day. At the moment I'm free most days. If I give you my phone number, you could ring me when you're free."

James smiled, "That would be great. Thanks."

* * * * *

"Mom, where are you," called her daughter Debbie.

"Upstairs, darling. Come up and let me know what you think about this new dress will you?"

Entering her mother's bedroom, Debbie whistled. "Wow, who is this gorgeous lady? What have you done with my mother?"

Looking at her daughter, Susie laughed. "Silly girl. What do you think? Does it look okay?"

"Is that for James?" Susie nodded her head. "Well, if that doesn't knock him off his feet, nothing will. You look a million dollars, mom."

"Thanks, sweetheart. Am I being stupid?"

Debbie looked at her mother. Since meeting James Haydon, she had blossomed into a new woman. And Debbie approved. Yes, she was sorry about her father, but he had treated her mom badly and she would never forgive him for what he had done to them both. "No, Mom, you are not being stupid. You like James, don't you?"

Watching her daughter's face, Susie replied, "Yes. He's very nice. I'd like to see more of him, but only if you agree it's okay."

"Hey, mom it's got nothing to do with me. I'm off to America soon to work. I'll feel a lot easier knowing you will have someone in your life who will take care of you. So, go for it. Anyway, what did the girls say?" By girls, Debbie was referring to the Musketeers.

"Just what you said – go for it," and Susie laughed.

Then turning to look at her image in the mirror she saw someone she hadn't seen for a long time. A happy woman. One who was attractive to a man who was considerate and caring of her every need. Debbie and the Musketeers were right – she should go for it – and she would.

www.ingramcontent.com/pod-product-compliance
Lightning Source LLC
Chambersburg PA
CBHW070654180626
46817CB00006B/2366